THE BLOTTING BOOK

Edward Frederick Benson was born on 24 July 1867 in Berkshire, the son of a future Archbishop of Canterbury, and one of six children. He studied at Kings College, Cambridge, and at the British School of Archaeology in Athens. Benson's first book, *Dodo*, was published to popular acclaim in 1893 and was followed by over a hundred books, including novels, histories, biographies and ghost stories. In 1920 Benson became a full-time tenant of Lamb House in Rye, which had once been home to the novelist Henry James. Rye provided the setting for Benson's popular 'Mapp and Lucia' stories and their author served three terms as mayor of Rye in the late 1930s. E. F. Benson died on 29 February 1940.

ALSO BY E. F. BENSON

E. F. BENSON

The Blotting Book

VINTAGE BOOKS
London

Published by Vintage 2013

2 4 6 8 10 9 7 5 3

First published in Great Britain by William Heinemann in 1908

Vintage
Random House, 20 Vauxhall Bridge Road,
London SW1V 2SA

www.vintage-books.co.uk

Addresses for companies within The Random House Group Limited can
be found at: www.randomhouse.co.uk/offices.htm

The Random House Group Limited Reg. No. 954009

A CIP catalogue record for this book
is available from the British Library

ISBN 9780099572428

The Random House Group Limited supports the Forest Stewardship
Council® (FSC®), the leading international forest-certification organisation.
Our books carrying the FSC label are printed on FSC®-certified paper.
FSC is the only forest-certification scheme supported by the leading
environmental organisations, including Greenpeace. Our
paper procurement policy can be found at
www.randomhouse.co.uk/environment

Typeset in Meridien by Replika Press Pvt Ltd, India

Printed and bound in Great Britain by
Clays Ltd, St Ives plc

Chapter I

MRS ASSHETON's house in Sussex Square, Brighton, was appointed with that finish of smooth stateliness which robs stateliness of its formality, and conceals the amount of trouble and personal attention which has, originally in any case, been spent on the production of the smoothness. Everything moved with the regularity of the solar system, and, superior to that wild rush of heavy bodies through infinite ether, there was never the slightest fear of comets streaking their unconjectured way across the sky, or meteorites falling on unsuspicious picnickers. In Mrs Assheton's house, supreme over climatic conditions, nobody ever felt that rooms were either too hot or too cold, a pleasantly fresh yet comfortably warm atmosphere pervaded the place, meals were always punctual and her admirable Scotch cook never served up a dish which, whether plain or ornate, was not, in its way, perfectly prepared. A couple of deft and noiseless parlour-maids attended to and anticipated the wants of her guests, from the moment they entered her hospitable doors

till when, on their leaving them, their coats were
held for them in the most convenient possible
manner for the easy insertion of the human arm,
and the tails of their dinner-coats cunningly and
unerringly tweaked from behind. In every way in
fact the house was an example of perfect comfort;
the softest carpets overlaid the floors, or, where
the polished wood was left bare, the parquetry
shone with a moonlike radiance; the newest and
most entertaining books (ready cut) stood on the
well-ordered shelves in the sitting-room to beguile
the leisure of the studiously minded; the billiard
table was always speckless of dust, no tip was ever
missing from any cue, and the cigarette boxes
and match-stands were always kept replenished.
In the dining-room the silver was resplendent,
until the moment when before dessert the cloth
was withdrawn, and showed a rosewood table that
might have served for a mirror to Narcissus.

Mrs Assheton, until her only surviving son Morris
had come to live with her some three months ago
on the completion of his four years at Cambridge,
had been alone, but even when she was alone this
ceremony of drawing the cloth and putting on the
dessert and wine had never been omitted, though
since she never took either, it might seem to be
a wasted piece of routine on the part of the two
noiseless parlour-maids. But she did not in the
least consider it so, for just as she always dressed
for dinner herself with the same care and finish,
whether she was going to dine alone or whether,
as tonight, a guest or two was dining with her, as

an offering, so to speak, on the altar of her own self-respect, so also she required self-respect and the formality that indicated it on the part of those who ministered at her table, and enjoyed such excellent wages. This pretty old-fashioned custom had always been the rule in her own home, and her husband had always had it practised during his life. And since then — his death had occurred some twenty years ago — nothing that she knew of had happened to make it less proper or desirable. Kind of heart and warm of soul though she was, she saw no reason for letting these excellent qualities cover any slackness or breach of observance in the social form of life to which she had been accustomed. There was no cause, because one was kind and wise, to eat with badly cleaned silver, unless the parlour-maid whose office it was to clean it was unwell. In such a case, if the extra work entailed by her illness would throw too much on the shoulders of the other servants, Mrs Assheton would willingly clean the silver herself, rather than that it should appear dull and tarnished. Her formalism, such as it was, was perfectly simple and sincere. She would, without any very poignant regret or sense of martyrdom, had her very comfortable income been cut down to a tenth of what it was, have gone to live in a four-roomed cottage with one servant. But she would have left that four-roomed cottage at once for even humbler surroundings had she found that her straitened circumstances did not permit her to keep it as speckless and *soignée* as was her present house in Sussex Square.

This achievement of having lived for nearly sixty years so decorously may perhaps be a somewhat finer performance than it sounds, but Mrs Assheton brought as her contribution to life in general a far finer offering than that, for though she did not propose to change her ways and manner of life herself, she was notoriously sympathetic with the changed life of the younger generation, and in consequence had the confidence of young folk generally. At this moment she was enjoying the fruits of her liberal attitude in the volubility of her son Morris, who sat at the end of the table opposite to her. His volubility was at present concerned with his motor-car, in which he had arrived that afternoon.

'Darling mother,' he was saying, 'I really was frightened as to whether you would mind. I couldn't help remembering how you received Mr Taynton's proposal that you should go for a drive in his car. Don't you remember, Mr Taynton? Mother's nose did go in the air. It's no use denying it. So I thought, perhaps, that she wouldn't like my having one. But I wanted it so dreadfully, and so I bought it without telling her, and drove down in it today, which is my birthday, so that she couldn't be too severe.'

Mr Taynton, while Morris was speaking, had picked up the nutcrackers the boy had been using, and was gravely exploding the shells of the nuts he had helped himself to. So Morris cracked the next one with a loud bang between his white even teeth.

'Dear Morris,' said his mother, 'how foolish of you. Give Mr Morris another nutcracker,' she added to the parlour-maid.

'What's foolish?' asked he, cracking another.

'Oh Morris, your teeth,' she said. 'Do wait a moment. Yes, that's right. And how can you say that my nose went in the air? I'm sure Mr Taynton will agree with me that that is really libellous. And as for your being afraid to tell me you had bought a motor-car yourself, why, that is sillier than cracking nuts with your teeth.'

Mr Taynton laughed a comfortable middle-aged laugh.

'Don't put the responsibility on me, Mrs Assheton,' he said. 'As long as Morris's bank doesn't tell us that his account is overdrawn, he can do what he pleases. But if we are told that, then down comes the cartloads of bricks.'

'Oh, you are a brick all right, Mr Taynton,' said the boy. 'I could stand a cartload of you.'

Mr Taynton, like his laugh, was comfortable and middle-aged. Solicitors are supposed to be sharp-faced and fox-like, but his face was well-furnished and comely, and his rather bald head beamed with benevolence and dinner.

'My dear boy,' he said, 'and it is your birthday — I cannot honour either you or this wonderful port more properly than by drinking your health in it.'

He began and finished his glass to the health he had so neatly proposed, and Morris laughed.

'Thank you very much,' he said. 'Mother, do send the port round. What an inhospitable woman!'

Mrs Assheton rose.

'I will leave you to be more hospitable than me, then, dear,' she said. 'Shall we go, Madge? Indeed, I am afraid you must, if you are to catch the train to Falmer.'

Madge Templeton got up with her hostess, and the two men rose too. She had been sitting next to Morris, and the boy looked at her eagerly.

'It's too bad, your having to go,' he said. 'But do you think I may come over tomorrow, in the afternoon some time, and see you and Lady Templeton? '

Madge paused a moment.

'I am so sorry,' she said, 'but we shall be away all day. We shan't be back till quite late.'

'Oh, what a bore,' said he, 'and I leave again on Friday. Do let me come and see you off then.'

But Mrs Assheton interposed.

'No, dear,' she said, 'I am going to have five minutes' talk with Madge before she goes and we don't want you. Look after Mr Taynton. I know he wants to talk to you and I want to talk to Madge.'

Mr Taynton, when the door had closed behind the ladies, sat down again with a rather obvious air of proposing to enjoy himself. It was quite true that he had a few pleasant things to say to Morris, it is also true that he immensely appreciated the wonderful port which glowed, ruby-like, in the nearly full decanter that lay to his hand. And, above all, he, with his busy life, occupied for the most part in innumerable small affairs, revelled in the sense of leisure and serene smoothness which permeated Mrs Assheton's house. He was still a year or two short of sixty, and but for his very bald and shining head would have seemed younger, so fresh was he in complexion, so active, despite a certain reassuring corpulency, was he in his movements. But when he dined quietly like this, at Mrs Assheton's, he would willingly have sacrificed the next five years of his life if he could have been assured on really reliable authority — the authority for instance of the Recording Angel — that in five years' time he would be able to sit quiet and not work any more. He wanted very much to be able to take a passive instead of an active interest in life, and this a few hundreds of pounds a year in addition to his savings would enable him to do. He saw, in fact, the goal arrived at which he would be able to sit still and wait with serenity and calmness for the event which would certainly relieve him of all further material anxieties. His very active life, the activities of which were so largely benevolent, had at the expiration of fifty-eight years a little tired him. He coveted the leisure which was so nearly his.

Morris lit a cigarette for himself, having previously passed the wine to Mr Taynton.

'I hate port,' he said, 'but my mother tells me this is all right. It was laid down the year I was born by the way. You don't mind my smoking, do you?'

This, to tell the truth, seemed almost sacrilegious

to Mr Taynton, for the idea that tobacco, especially the frivolous cigarette, should burn in a room where such port was being drunk was sheer crime against human and divine laws. But he could scarcely indicate to his host that he should not smoke in his own dining-room.

'No, my dear Morris,' he said, 'but really you almost shock me, when you prefer tobacco to this nectar, I assure you nectar. And the car, now, tell me more about the car.'

Morris laughed.

'I'm so deeply thankful I haven't overdrawn,' he said. 'Oh, the car's a clipper. We came down from Haywards Heath the most gorgeous pace. I saw one policeman trying to take my number, but we raised such a dust, I don't think he can have been able to see it. It's such rot only going twenty miles an hour with a clear straight road ahead.'

Mr Taynton sighed, gently and not unhappily.

'Yes, yes, my dear boy, I so sympathise with you,' he said. 'Speed and violence is the proper attitude of youth, just as strength with a more measured pace, is the proper gait for older folk. And that, I fancy, is just what Mrs Assheton felt. She would feel it to be as unnatural in you to care to drive with her in her very comfortable victoria as she would feel it to be unnatural in herself to wish to go in your lightning speed motor. And that reminds me. As your trustee——'

Coffee was brought in at this moment, carried, not by one of the discreet parlour-maids, but by a young man-servant. Mr Taynton, with the port still by him, refused it, but looked rather curiously at the servant. Morris however mixed himself a cup in which cream, sugar, and coffee were about equally mingled.

'A new servant of your mother's?' he asked, when the man had left the room.

'Oh no. It's my man, Martin. Awfully handy chap. Cleans silver, boots and the motor. Drives it, too, when I'll let him, which isn't very often. Chauffeurs are such rotters, aren't they? Regular chauffeurs I mean. They always make out that something is wrong with the car, just as dentists always find some hole in your teeth, if you go to them.'

Mr Taynton did not reply to these critical generalities but went back to what he had been saying when the entry of coffee interrupted him.

'As your mother said,' he remarked, 'I wanted to have a few words with you. You are twenty-two, are you not, today? Well, when I was young we considered anyone of twenty-two a boy still, but now I think young fellows grow up more quickly, and at twenty-two, you are a man nowadays, and I think it is time for you, since my trusteeship for you may end any day now, to take a rather more active interest in the state of your finances than you have hitherto done. I want you in fact, my dear fellow, to listen to me for five minutes while I state your position to you.'

Morris indicated the port again, and Mr Taynton refilled his glass.

'I have had twenty years of stewardship for you,'

he went on, 'and before my stewardship comes to an end, which it will do anyhow in three years from now, and may come to an end any day——'

'Why, how is that?' asked Morris.

'If you marry, my dear boy. By the terms of your father's will, your marriage, provided it takes place with your mother's consent, and after your twenty-second birthday, puts you in complete control and possession of your fortune. Otherwise, as of course you know, you come of age, legally speaking, on your twenty-fifth birthday.'

Morris lit another cigarette rather impatiently.

'Yes, I knew I was a minor till I was twenty-five,' he said, 'and I suppose I have known that if I married after the age of twenty-two, I became a major, or whatever you call it. But what then? Do let us go and play billiards, I'll give you twenty-five in a hundred, because I've been playing a lot lately, and I'll bet half a crown.'

Mr Taynton's fist gently tapped the table.

'Done,' he said, 'and we will play in five minutes. But I have something to say to you first. Your mother, as you know, enjoys the income of the bulk of your father's property for her lifetime. Outside that, he left this much smaller capital of which, as also of her money, my partner and I are trustees. The sum he left you was thirty thousand pounds. It is now rather over forty thousand pounds, since we have changed the investments from time to time, and always, I am glad to say, with satisfactory results. The value of her property has gone up also in a corresponding degree. That, however, does not concern you. But since you are now twenty-two, and your marriage would put the whole of this smaller sum into your hands, would it not be well for you to look through our books, to see for yourself the account we render of our stewardship?'

Morris laughed.

'But for what reason?' he asked. 'You tell me that my portion has increased in value by ten thousand pounds. I am delighted to hear it. And I thank you very much. And as for——'

He broke off short, and Mr Taynton let a perceptible pause follow before he interrupted.

'As for the possibility of your marrying?' he suggested.

Morris gave him a quick, eager, glance.

'Yes, I think there is that possibility,' he said. 'I hope — I hope it is not far distant.'

'My dear boy——' said the lawyer.

'Ah, not a word. I don't know——'

Morris pushed his chair back quickly, and stood up — his tall slim figure outlined against the sober red of the dining-room wall. A plume of black hair had escaped from his well-brushed head and hung over his forehead, and his sun-tanned vivid face looked extraordinarily handsome. His mother's clear-cut energetic features were there, with the glow and buoyancy of youth kindling them. Violent vitality was his also; his was the hot blood that could do any deed when the life-instinct commanded it. He looked like one of those who could give their body to be burned in the pursuit of an idea, or could as easily steal, or kill, provided only the deed

was vitally done in the heat of his blood. Violence
was clearly his mode of life: the motor had to go
sixty miles an hour; he might be one of those
who bathed in the Serpentine in mid-winter; he
would clearly dance all night, and ride all day, and
go on till he dropped in the pursuit of what he
cared for. Mr Taynton, looking at him as he stood
smiling there, in his splendid health and vigour,
felt all this. He felt, too, that if Morris intended to
be married tomorrow morning, matrimony would
probably take place.

But Morris's pause, after he pushed his chair
back and stood up, was only momentary.

'Good God, yes; I'm in love,' he said. 'And she
probably thinks me a stupid barbarian, who likes
only to drive golfballs and motor-cars. She — oh,
it's hopeless. She would have let me come over to
see them tomorrow otherwise.'

He paused again.

'And now I've given the whole show away,' he
said.

Mr Taynton made a comfortable sort of noise.
It was compounded of laughter, sympathy, and
comprehension.

'You gave it away long ago, my dear Morris,'
he said.

'You had guessed?' asked Morris, sitting down
again with the same quickness and violence of
movement, and putting both his elbows on the
table.

'No, my dear boy, you had told me, as you
have told everybody, without mentioning it. And I

most heartily congratulate you. I never saw a more delightful girl. Professionally also, I feel bound to add that it seems to me a most proper alliance — heirs should always marry heiresses. It' — Mr Taynton drank off the rest of his port — 'it keeps properties together.'

Hot blood again dictated to Morris: it seemed dreadful to him that any thought of money or of property could be mentioned in the same breath as that which he longed for. He rose again as abruptly and violently as he had sat down.

'Well, let's play billiards,' he said. 'I — I don't think you understand a bit. You can't, in fact.'

Mr Taynton stroked the tablecloth for a moment with a plump white forefinger.

'Crabbed age and youth,' he remarked. 'But crabbed age makes an appeal to youth, if youth will kindly call to mind what crabbed age referred to some five minutes ago. In other words, will you, or will you not, Morris, spend a very dry three hours at my office, looking into the account of my stewardship? There was thirty thousand pounds, and there now is — or should we say 'are' — forty. It will take you not less than two hours, and not more than three. But since my stewardship may come to an end, as I said, any day, I should, not for my own sake, but for yours, wish you to see what we have done for you, and — I own this would be a certain private gratification to me — to learn that you thought that the trust your dear father reposed in us was not misplaced.'

There was something about these simple words

which touched Morris. For the moment he became
almost businesslike. Mr Taynton had been, as he
knew, a friend of his father's, and, as he had said,
he had been steward of his own affairs for twenty
years. But that reflection banished the businesslike
view.

'Oh, but two hours is a fearful time,' he said.
'You have told me the facts, and they entirely satisfy
me. And I want to be out all day tomorrow, as I
am only here till the day after. But I shall be down
again next week. Let us go into it all then. Not that
there is the slightest use in going into anything.
And when, Mr Taynton, I become steward of my
own affairs, you may be quite certain that I shall
beg you to continue looking after them. Why you
gained me ten thousand pounds in these twenty
years — I wonder what there would have been to
my credit now if I had looked after things myself.
But since we are on the subject I should like just
this once to assure you of my great gratitude to
you, for all you have done. And I ask you, if you
will, to look after my affairs in the future with the
same completeness as you have always done. My
father's will does not prevent that, does it?'

Mr Taynton looked at the young fellow with
affection.

'Dear Morris,' he said gaily, 'we lawyers and
solicitors are always supposed to be sharks, but
personally I am not such a shark as that. Are you
aware that I am paid £200 a year for my stewardship,
which you are entitled to assume for yourself on
your marriage, though of course its continuance

in my hands is not forbidden in your father's will? You are quite competent to look after your affairs yourself; it is ridiculous for you to continue to pay me this sum. But I thank you from the bottom of my heart for your confidence in me.'

A very close observer might have seen that behind Mr Taynton's kind gay eyes there was sitting a personality, so to speak, that, as his mouth framed these words, was watching Morris rather narrowly and anxiously. But the moment Morris spoke this silent secret watcher popped back again out of sight.

'Well then I ask you as a personal favour,' said he, 'to continue being my steward. Why, it's good business for me, isn't it? In twenty years you make me ten thousand pounds, and I only pay you £200 a year for it. Please be kind, Mr Taynton, and continue making me rich. Oh, I'm a jolly hard-headed chap really; I know that it is to my advantage.'

Mr Taynton considered this a moment, playing with his wine glass. Then he looked up quickly.

'Yes, Morris, I will with pleasure do as you ask me,' he said.

'Right oh. Thanks awfully. Do come and play billiards.'

Morris was in amazing luck that night, and if, as he said, he had been playing a lot lately, the advantage of his practice was seen chiefly in the hideous certainty of his flukes, and the game (though he received twenty-five) left Mr Taynton half a crown the poorer. Then the winner whirled his guest upstairs again to talk to his mother while he himself went round to the stables to assure himself of the well-being of the beloved motor. Martin had already valeted it, after its run, and was just locking up when Morris arrived.

Morris gave his orders for next day after a quite unnecessary examination into the internal economy of the beloved, and was just going back to the house, when he paused, remembering something.

'Oh Martin,' he said, 'while I am here, I want you to help in the house, you know at dinner and so on, just as you did tonight. And when there are guests of mine here I want you to look after them. For instance, when Mr Taynton goes tonight you will be there to give him his hat and coat. You'll have rather a lot to do, I'm afraid.'

Morris finished his cigarette and went back to the drawing-room where Mr Taynton was already engaged in the staid excitements of backgammon with his mother. That game over, Morris took his place, and before long the lawyer rose to go.

'Now I absolutely refuse to let you interrupt your game,' he said. 'I have found my way out of this house often enough, I should think. Good night, Mrs Assheton. Good night, Morris; don't break your neck my dear boy, in trying to break records.'

Morris hardly attended to this, for the game was critical. He just rang the bell, said good night, and had thrown again before the door had closed behind Mr Taynton. Below, in answer to the bell, was standing his servant.

Mr Taynton looked at him again with some attention, and then glanced round to see if the discreet parlour-maids were about.

'So you are called Martin now,' he observed gently.

'Yes, sir.'

'I recognised you at once.'

There was a short pause.

'Are you going to tell Mr Morris, sir?' he asked.

'That I had to dismiss you two years ago for theft?' said Mr Taynton quietly. 'No, not if you behave yourself.'

Mr Taynton looked at him again kindly and sighed.

'No, let bygones be bygones,' he said. 'You will find your secret is safe enough. And, Martin, I hope you have really turned over a new leaf, and are living honestly now. That is so, my lad? Thank God; thank God. My umbrella? Thanks. Good night. No cab: I will walk.'

Chapter II

MR TAYNTON lived in a square, comfortable house in Montpellier Road, and thus, when he left Mrs Assheton's there was some two miles of pavement and sea front between him and home. But the night was of wonderful beauty, a night of mid-June, warm enough to make the most cautious secure of chill, and at the same time just made crisp with a little breeze that blew or rather whispered landward from over the full-tide of the sleeping sea. High up in the heavens swung a glorious moon, which cast its path of white enchanted light over the ripples, and seemed to draw the heart even as it drew the eyes heavenward. Mr Taynton certainly, as he stepped out beneath the stars, with the sea lying below him, felt, in his delicate and sensitive nature, the charm of the hour, and being a good if not a brisk walker, he determined to go home on foot. And he stepped westward very contentedly.

The evening, it would appear, had much pleased him — for it was long before his smile of retrospective pleasure faded from his pleasant mobile face. Morris's trust and confidence in him had been extraordinarily pleasant to him: and modest and unassuming as he was, he could not help a secret gratification at the thought. What a handsome fellow Morris was too, how gay, how attractive! He had his father's dark colouring, and tall figure, but much of his mother's grace and charm had gone to the modelling of that thin sensitive mouth and the long oval of his face. Yet there was more of the father there, the father's intense, almost violent, vitality was somehow more characteristic of the essential Morris than face or feature.

What a happy thing it was too — here the smile of pleasure illuminated Mr Taynton's face again — that the boy whom he had dismissed two years before for some petty pilfering in his own house, should have turned out such a promising lad and should have found his way to so pleasant a berth as that of factotum to Morris. Kindly and charitable all through and ever eager to draw out the good in everybody and forgive the bad, Mr Taynton had often occasion to deplore the hardness and uncharity of a world which remembers youthful errors and hangs them, like a mill-stone, round the neck of the offender, and it warmed his heart and kindled his smile to think of one case at any rate where a youthful misdemeanour was lived down and forgotten. At the time he remembered being in doubt whether he should not give the offender up to justice, for the pilfering, petty though it had been, had been somewhat persistent, but he had taken the more merciful course, and merely dismissed the boy. He had been in two minds about it before, wondering whether it would not be better to let Martin have a sharp lesson, but tonight he was thankful that he had not done so. The mercy he had shown had come back to bless him also; he felt a glow of thankfulness that the subject of his clemency had turned out so well. Punishment often hardens the criminal, was one of his settled convictions. But Morris — again his thoughts went back to Morris, who was already standing on the verge of manhood, on the verge, too, he made no doubt, of married life and its joys and responsibilities. Mr Taynton was himself a bachelor, and the thought gave him not a moment of jealousy, but a moment of void that ached a little at the thought of the common human bliss which he had himself missed. How charming, too, was the girl Madge Templeton, whom he had met, not for the first time, that evening. He himself had guessed how things stood between the two before Morris had confided in him, and it pleased him that his intuition was confirmed. What a pity, however, that the two were not going to meet next day, that she was out with her mother and would not get back till late. It would have been a cooling thought in the hot office hours of tomorrow to picture them sitting together in the garden at Falmer, or under one of the cool deep-foliaged oaks in the park.

Then suddenly his face changed, the smile faded, but came back next instant and broadened with a laugh. And the man who laughs when he is by himself may certainly be supposed to have strong cause for amusement.

Mr Taynton had come by this time to the West Pier, and a hundred yards farther would bring him to Montpellier Road. But it was yet early, as he saw (so bright was the moonlight) when he consulted his watch, and he retraced his steps some fifty yards, and eventually rang at the door of a big house of flats facing the sea, where his partner, who for the most part, looked after the London branch of their business, had his *pied-à-terre*. Eor the firm of Taynton and Mills was one of those respectable and solid businesses that, beginning in the country, had eventually been extended to town, and so far from its having its headquarters in town and its branch in Brighton, had its headquarters here and its branch in the metropolis. Mr Godfrey Mills, so he learned at the door had dined alone, and was in, and without further delay Mr Taynton was carried aloft in the gaudy bird-cage of the lift, feeling sure that his partner would see him.

The flat into which he was ushered with a smile of welcome from the man who opened the door was furnished with a sort of gross opulence that never failed to jar on Mr Taynton's exquisite taste and cultivated mind. Pictures, chairs, sofas, the patterns of the carpet, and the heavy gilding of the cornices were all sensuous, a sort of frangipani to the eye. The apparent contrast, however, between these things and their owner, was as great as that between Mr Taynton and his partner, for Mr Godfrey Mills was a thin, spare, dark little man, brisk in movement, with a look in his eye that betokened a watchfulness and vigilance of the most alert order. But useful as such a gift undoubtedly is, it was given to Mr Godfrey Mills perhaps a shade too obviously. It would be unlikely that the stupidest or shallowest person would give himself away when talking to him, for it was so clear that he was always on the watch for admission or information that might be useful to him. He had, however, the charm that a very active and vivid mind always possesses, and though small and slight, he was a figure that would be noticed anywhere, so keen and wide-awake was his face. Beside him Mr Taynton looked like a benevolent country clergyman, more distinguished for amiable qualities of the heart, than intellectual qualities of the head. Yet those — there were not many of them — who in dealings with the latter had tried to conduct their business on these assumptions, had invariably found it necessary to reconsider their first impression of him. His partner, however, was always conscious of a little impatience in talking to him; Taynton, he would have allowed, did not lack fine business qualities, but he was a little wanting in quickness.

Mills's welcome of him was abrupt.

'Pleased to see you,' he said. 'Cigar, drink? Sit down, won't you? What is it?'

'I dropped in for a chat on my way home,' said Mr Taynton. 'I have been dining with Mrs Assheton. A most pleasant evening. What a fine delicate face she has.'

Mills bit off the end of a cigar.

'I take it that you did not come in merely to discuss the delicacy of Mrs Assheton's face,' he said.

'No, no, dear fellow; you are right to recall me. I too take it — I take it that you have found time to go over to Falmer yesterday. How did you find Sir Richard?'

'I found him well. I had a long talk with him.'

'And you managed to convey something of those very painful facts which you felt it was your duty to bring to his notice?' asked Mr Taynton.

Godfrey Mills laughed.

'I say, Taynton, is it really worth while keeping it up like this?' he asked. 'It really saves so much trouble to talk straight, as I propose to do. I saw him, as I said, and I really managed remarkably well. I had these admissions wrung from me, I assure you it is no less than that, under promise of the most absolute secrecy. I told him young Assheton was leading an idle, extravagant, and dissipated life. I said I had seen him three nights ago in Piccadilly, not quite sober, in company with the class of person to whom one does not refer in polite society. Will that do?'

'Ah, I can easily imagine how painful you must have found——' began Taynton.

But his partner interrupted.

'It was rather painful; you have spoken a true word in jest. I felt a brute, I tell you. But, as I pointed out to you, something of the sort was necessary.'

Mr Taynton suddenly dropped his slightly clerical manner.

'You have done excellently, my dear friend,' he said. 'And as you pointed out to me, it was indeed necessary to do something of the sort. I think by now, your revelations have already begun to take effect. Yes, I think I will take a little brandy and soda. Thank you very much.'

He got up with greater briskness than he had hitherto shown.

'And you are none too soon,' he said. 'Morris, poor Morris, such a handsome fellow, confided to me this evening that he was in love with Miss Templeton. He is very much in earnest.'

'And why do you think my interview has met with some success?' asked Mills.

'Well, it is only a conjecture, but when Morris asked if he might call any time tomorrow, Miss Templeton (who was also dining with Mrs Assheton) said that she and her mother would be out all day and not get home till late. It does not strike me as being too fanciful to see in that some little trace perhaps of your handiwork.'

'Yes, that looks like me,' said Mills shortly.

Mr Taynton took a meditative sip at his brandy and soda.

'My evening also has not been altogether wasted,' he said. 'I played what for me was a bold stroke, for as you know, my dear fellow, I prefer to leave to your nimble and penetrating mind things that want dash and boldness. But tonight, yes, I was warmed with that wonderful port and was bold.'

'What did you do?' asked Mills.

'Well, I asked, I almost implored dear Morris to give me two or three hours tomorrow and go through all the books, and satisfy himself everything is in order, and his investments well looked after. I told him also that the original £30,000 of his had, owing to judicious management, become £40,000. You see, that is unfortunately a thing past praying for. It is so indubitably clear from the earlier ledgers——'

'But the port must indeed have warmed you,' said Mills quickly. 'Why, it was madness! What if he had consented?'

Mr Taynton smiled.

'Ah, well, I in my slow synthetic manner had made up my mind that it was really quite impossible that he should consent to go into the books and vouchers. To begin with, he has a new motor car, and every hour spent away from that car just now is to his mind an hour wasted. Also, I know him well. I knew that he would never consent to spend several hours over ledgers. Finally, even if he had, though I knew from what I know of him not that he would not but that he *could* not, I could have — I could have managed something. You see, he know nothing whatever about business or investments.'

Mills shook his head.

'But it was dangerous, anyhow,' he said, 'and I don't understand what object could be served by it. It was running a risk with no profit in view.'

Then for the first time the inherent strength of the quietness of the one man as opposed to the obvious quickness and comprehension of the other came into play.

'I think that I disagree with you there, my dear fellow,' said Mr Taynton slowly, 'though when I have told you all, I shall be of course, as always, delighted to recognise the superiority of your judgment, should you disagree with me, and convince me of the correctness of your view. It has happened, I know, a hundred times before that you with your quick intuitive perceptions have been right.'

But his partner interrupted him. He quite agreed with the sentiment, but he wanted to learn without even the delay caused by these complimentary remarks, the upshot of Taynton's rash proposal to Morris.

'What did young Assheton say?' he asked.

'Well, my dear fellow,' said Taynton, 'though I have really no doubt that in principle I did a rash thing, in actual practice my step was justified, because Morris absolutely refused to look at the books. Of course I know the young fellow well: it argues no perspicuity on my part to have foreseen that. And, I am glad to say, something in my way of putting it, some sincerity of manner I suppose, gave rise to a fresh mark of confidence in us on his part.'

Mr Taynton cleared his throat; his quietness and complete absence of hurry was, so to speak, rapidly overhauling the quick, nimble mind of the other.

'He asked me in fact to continue being steward of his affairs in any event. Should he marry tomorrow I feel no doubt that he would not spend a couple of minutes over his financial affairs, unless, *unless*, as you foresaw might happen, he had need of a large lump sum. In that case, my dear Mills, you and I would — would find it impossible to live elsewhere than in the Argentine Republic, were we so fortunate as to get there. But, as far as this goes I only say that the step of mine which you felt to be dangerous has turned out most auspiciously. He begged me, in fact, to continue even after he came of age, acting for him at my present rate of remuneration.'

Mr Mills was listening to this with some attention. Here he laughed dryly.

'That is capital, then,' he said. 'You were right and I was wrong. God, Taynton, it's your manner you know, there's something of the country parson about you that is wonderfully convincing. You seem sincere without being sanctimonious. Why, if I was to ask young Assheton to look into his affairs for himself, he would instantly think there was something wrong, and that I was trying bluff. But when you do the same thing, that simple and perfectly correct explanation never occurs to him.'

'No, dear Morris trusts me very completely,' said Taynton, 'But. then, if I may continue my little review of the situation, as it now stands, you and your talk with Sir Richard have vastly decreased the danger of his marrying. For, to be frank, I should not feel at all secure if that happened. Miss Templeton is an heiress herself, and Morris might easily take it into his head to spend ten or fifteen thousand pounds in building a house or buying an estate, and though I think I have guarded against his requiring an account of our stewardship, I can't prevent his wishing to draw a large sum of money. But your brilliant manœuvre may, we hope, effectually put a stop to the danger of his marrying Miss Templeton, and since I am convinced he is in love with her, why' — Mr Taynton put his plump finger-tips together and raised his kind eyes to the ceiling — 'why, the chance of his wanting to marry anybody else is postponed anyhow, till, till he has got over this unfortunate attachment. In fact, my dear fellow, there is no longer anything immediate to fear, and I feel sure that before many weeks are up, the misfortunes and ill luck which for the last two years have dogged us with such incredible persistency will be repaired.'

Mills said nothing for the moment but splashed himself out a liberal allowance of brandy into his glass, and mixed it with a somewhat more carefully measured ration of soda. He was essentially a sober man, but that was partly due to the fact that his head was as impervious to alcohol as teak is to water, and it was his habit to indulge in two, and those rather stiff, brandies and sodas of an evening. He found that they assisted and clarified thought.

'I wish to heaven you hadn't found it necessary

to let young Assheton know that his £30,000 had increased to £40,000,' he said. 'That's £10,000 more to get back.'

'Ah, it was just that which gave him, so he thought, such good cause for reposing complete confidence in me,' remarked Mr Taynton. 'But as you say, it is £10,000 more to get back, and I should not have told him, were not certain ledgers of earlier years so extremely, extremely unmistakable on the subject.'

'But if he is not going to look at ledgers at all——' began Mills.

'Ah, the concealment of that sort of thing is one of the risks which it is not worth while to take,' said the other, dropping for a moment the deferential attitude.

Mills was silent again. Then:

'Have you bought that option in Boston Coppers?' he asked.

'Yes; I bought today.'

Mills glanced at the clock as Mr Taynton rose to go.

'Still only a quarter to twelve,' he said. 'If you have time, you might give me a detailed statement. I hardly know what you have done. It won't take a couple of minutes.'

Mr Taynton glanced at the clock likewise, and then put down his hat again.

'I can just spare the time,' he said, 'but I must get home by twelve; I have unfortunately come out without my latchkey, and I do not like keeping the servants up.'

He pressed his fingers over his eyes a moment and then spoke.

Ten minutes later he was in the bird-cage of the lift again, and by twelve he had been admitted into his own house, apologising most amiably to his servant for having kept him up. There were a few letters for him and he opened and read those, then lit his bed-candle and went upstairs, but instead of undressing, sat for a full quarter of an hour in his armchair thinking. Then he spoke softly to himself.

'I think dear Mills means mischief in some way,' he said. 'But really for the moment it puzzles me to know what. However, I shall see tomorrow. Ah, I wonder if I guess!'

Then he went to bed, but contrary to custom did not get to sleep for a long time. But when he did there was a smile on his lips; a patient contented smile.

Chapter III

MR TAYNTON's statement to his partner, which had taken him so few minutes to give, was of course concerned only with the latest financial operation which he had just embarked in, but for the sake of the reader it will be necessary to go a little further back, and give quite shortly the main features of the situation in which he and his partner found themselves placed.

Briefly then, just two years ago, at the time peace was declared in South Africa, the two partners of Taynton and Mills had sold out £30,000 of Morris Assheton's securities, which owing to their excellent management was then worth £40,000, and seeing a quite unrivalled opportunity of making their fortunes, had become heavy purchasers of South African mines, for they reasoned that with peace once declared it was absolutely certain that prices would go up. But, as is sometimes the way with absolute certainties, the opposite had happened and they had gone down. They cut their loss, however, and proceeded to buy American rails. In six months they had entirely repaired the damage, and seeing further unrivalled opportunities from time to time, in buying motor-car shares, in running a theatre and other schemes, had managed a month ago to lose all that was left of the £30,000. Being, therefore, already so deeply committed, it was mere prudence, the mere instinct of self-preservation that had led them to sell out the remaining £10,000, and today Mr Taynton had bought an option in Boston copper with it. The manner of an option is as follows:

Boston Copper today was quoted at £5 10s 6d, and by paying a premium of twelve shillings and sixpence per share, they were entitled to buy Boston Copper shares any time within the next three months at a price of £6 3s. Supposing therefore (as Mr Taynton on very good authority had supposed) that Boston Copper, a rapidly improving company, rose a couple of points within the next three months, and so stood at £7 10s 6d; he had the right of exercising his option and buying them at £6 3s thus making £1 7s 6d per share. But a higher rise than this was confidently expected, and Taynton, though not really of an over sanguine disposition, certainly hoped to make good the greater part if not all of their somewhat large defalcations. He had bought an option of 20,000 shares, the option of which cost (or would cost at the end of those months) rather over £10,000. In other words, the moment that the shares rose to a price higher than £6 3s, all further appreciation was pure gain. If they did not rise so high, he would of course not exercise the option, and sacrifice the money.

That was certainly a very unpleasant thing to contemplate, but it had been more unpleasant when, so far as he knew, Morris was on the verge of matrimony, and would then step into the management of his own affairs. But bad though it all was, the situation had certainly been immensely ameliorated this evening, since on the one hand his partner had, it was not unreasonable to hope, said to Madge's father things about Morris that made his marriage with Madge exceedingly unlikely, while on the other hand, even if it happened, his affairs, according to his own wish, would remain in Mr Taynton's hands with the same completeness as heretofore. It would, of course, be necessary to pay him his income, and though this would be a great strain on the finances of the two partners, it was manageable. Besides (Mr Taynton sincerely hoped that this would not be necessary) the money which was Mrs Assheton's for her lifetime was in his hands also, so if the worst came to the worst——

Now the composition and nature of the extraordinary animal called man is so unexpected and unlikely that any analysis of Mr Taynton's character may seem almost grotesque. It is a fact nevertheless that his was a nature capable of great things, it is also a fact that he had long ago been deeply and bitterly contrite for the original dishonesty of using the money of his client. But by aid of those strange perversities of nature, he had by this time honestly and sincerely got to regard all their subsequent employments of it merely as efforts on his part to make right an original wrong. He wanted to repair his fault, and it seemed to him that to commit it again was the only means at his disposal for doing so. A strain, too, of Puritan piety was bound up in the constitution of his soul, and in private life he exercised high morality, and was also kind and charitable. He belonged to guilds and societies that had as their object the improvement and moral advancement of young men. He was a liberal patron of educational schemes, he sang a fervent and fruity tenor in the choir of St Agnes, he was a regular communicant, his nature looked toward good, and turned its eyes away from evil. To do him justice he was not a hypocrite, though, if all about him were known, and a plebiscite taken, it is probable that he would be unanimously condemned. Yet the universal opinion would be wrong: he was no hypocrite, but only had the bump of self-preservation enormously developed. He had cheated and swindled, but he was genuinely opposed to cheating and swindling. He was cheating and swindling now, in buying the option of Boston Copper. But he did not know that: he wanted to repair the original wrong, to hand back to Morris his fortune unimpaired and also to save himself. But of these two wants, the second, it must be confessed, was infinitely the stronger. To save himself there was perhaps nothing that he would stick at. However, it was his constant wish and prayer that he might not be led into temptation. He knew well what his particular temptation was, namely this instinct of self-preservation, and constantly thought and meditated about it. He knew that he was hardly himself when the stress of it came on him; it was like a possession.

Mills, though an excellent partner and a man of most industrious habits, had, so Mr Taynton would have admitted, one little weak spot. He never was at the office till rather late in the morning. True, when he came, he soon made up for lost time, for he was possessed, as we have seen, of a notable quickness and agility of mind, but sometimes Taynton found that he was himself forced to be idle till Mills turned up, if his signature or what not was required for papers before work could be further proceeded with. This, in fact, was the case next morning, and from half past eleven Mr Taynton had to sit idly in his office, as far as the work of the firm was concerned, until his partner arrived. It was a little tiresome that this should happen today, because there was nothing else that need detain him, except those deeds for the execution of which his partner's signature was necessary, and he could, if only Mills had been punctual, have gone out to Rottingdean before lunch, and inspected the Church school there in the erection of which he had taken so energetic an interest. Timmins, however, the grey-haired old head clerk, was in the office with him, and Mr Taynton always liked a chat with Timmins.

'And the grandson just come home, has he, Mr Timmins?' he was saying. 'I must come and see him. Why he'll be six years old, won't he, by now?'

'Yes, sir, turned six.'

'Dear me, how time goes on! The morning is going on, too, and still Mr Mills isn't here.'

He took a quill pen and drew a half sheet of paper toward him, poised his pen a moment and then wrote quickly.

'What a pity I can't sign for him,' he said, passing his paper over to the clerk. 'Look at that; now even you, Timmins, though you have seen Mr Mills's handwriting ten thousand times, would be ready to swear that the signature was his, would you not?'

Timmins looked scrutinisingly at it.

'Well, I'm sure, sir! What a forger you would have made!' he said admiringly. 'I would have sworn that was Mr Mills's own hand of write. It's wonderful, sir.'

Mr Taynton sighed, and took the paper again.

'Yes, it is like, isn't it?' he said, 'and it's so easy to do. Luckily forgers don't know the way to forge properly.'

'And what might that be, sir?' asked Timmins.

'Why, to throw yourself mentally into the nature of the man whose handwriting you wish to forge. Of course one has to know the handwriting thoroughly well, but if one does that one just has to visualise it, and then, as I said, project oneself into the other, not laboriously copy the handwriting. Let's try another. Ah, who is that letter from? Mrs Assheton isn't it. Let me look at the signature just once again.'

Mr Taynton closed his eyes a moment after looking at it. Then he took his quill, and wrote quickly.

'You would swear to that, too, would you not, Timmins?' he asked.

'Why, God bless me yes, sir,' said he. 'Swear to it on the book.'

The door opened and as Godfrey Mills came in, Mr Taynton tweaked the paper out of Timmins's hand, and tore it up. It might perhaps seem strange to dear Mills that his partner had been forging his signature, though only in jest.

''Fraid I'm rather late,' said Mills.

'Not at all, my dear fellow,' said Taynton without the slightest touch of ill-humour. 'How are you? There's very little to do; I want your signature to this and this, and your careful perusal of that. Mrs Assheton's letter? No, that only concerns me; I have dealt with it.'

A quarter of an hour was sufficient, and at the end Timmins carried the papers away leaving the two partners together. Then, as soon as the door closed, Mills spoke.

'I've been thinking over our conversation of last night,' he said, 'and there are some points I don't think you have quite appreciated, which I should like to put before you.'

Something inside Mr Taynton's brain, the same watcher perhaps who looked at Morris so closely the evening before, said to him: 'He is going to try it on.' But it was not the watcher but his normal self that answered. He beamed gently on his partner.

'My dear fellow, I might have been sure that your quick mind would have seen new aspects, new combinations,' he said.

Mills leaned forward over the table.

'Yes, I have seen new aspects, to adopt your words,' he said, 'and I will put them before you. These financial operations, shall we call them, have been going on for two years now, have they not? You began by losing a large sum in South Africans——'

'We began,' corrected Mr Taynton, gently. He was looking at the other quite calmly; his face expressed no surprise at all; if there was anything in his expression beyond that of quiet kindness, it was perhaps pity.

'I said "you" ,' said Mills in a hectoring tone, 'and I will soon explain why. You lost a large sum in South Africans, but won it back again in Americans. You then again, and again contrary to my advice, embarked in perfect wild-cat affairs, which ended in our – I say 'our' here – getting severely scratched and mauled. Altogether you have frittered away £30,000, and have placed the remaining ten in a venture which to my mind is as wild as all the rest of your unfortunate ventures. These speculations have, almost without exception, been choices of your own, not mine. That was *one* of the reasons why I said "you", not "we" .'

He paused a moment.

'Another reason is,' he said, 'because without any exception the transactions have taken place on your advice and in your name, not in mine.'

That was a sufficiently meaning statement, but Mills did not wish his partner to be under any misapprehension as to what he implied.

'In other words,' he said, 'I can deny absolutely all knowledge of the whole of those operations.'

Mr Taynton gave a sudden start, as if the significance of this had only this moment dawned on him, as if he had not understood the first statement. Then he seemed to collect himself.

'You can hardly do that,' he said, 'as I hold letters of yours which imply such knowledge.'

Mills smiled rather evilly.

'Ah, it is not worth while bluffing,' he said. 'I have never written such a letter to you. You know it. Is it likely I should?'

Mr Taynton apparently had no reply to this. But he had a question to ask.

'Why are you taking up this hostile and threatening attitude?'

'I have not meant to be hostile, and I have certainly not threatened,' replied Mills. 'I have put before you, quite dispassionately I hope, certain facts. Indeed I should say it was you who had threatened in the matter of those letters, which, unhappily, have never existed at all. I will proceed.

'Now what has been my part in this affair? I have observed you lost money in speculations of which I disapproved, but you always knew best. I have advanced money to you before now to tide over embarrassments that would otherwise have been disastrous. By the exercise of diplomacy — or lying — yesterday, I averted a very grave danger. I point out to you also that there is nothing to implicate me in these — these fraudulent employments of a client's money. So I ask, where do I come in? What do I get by it?'

Mr Taynton's hands were trembling as he fumbled at some papers on his desk.

'You know quite well that we are to share all profits?' he said.

'Yes, but at present there have not been any. I have been, to put it plainly, pulling you out of holes. And I think — I think my trouble ought to be remunerated. I sincerely hope you will take that view also. Or shall I remind you again that there is nothing in the world to connect me with these, well, frauds?'

Mr Taynton got up from his chair, strolled across to the window where he drew down the blind a little, so as to shut out the splash of sunlight that fell on his table.

'You have been betting again, I suppose,' he asked quietly.

'Yes, and have been unfortunate. Pray do not trouble to tell me again how foolish it is to gamble like that. You may be right. I have no doubt you are right. But I think one has as much right to gamble with one's own money as to do so with the money of other people.'

This apparently seemed unanswerable; anyhow Mr Taynton made no reply. Then, having excluded the splash of sunlight he sat down again.

'You have not threatened, you tell me,' he said,

'but you have pointed out to me that there is no evidence that you have had a hand in certain transactions. You say that I know you have helped me in these transactions; you say you require remuneration for your services. Does not that, I ask, imply a threat? Does it not mean that you are blackmailing me? Else why should you bring these facts — I do not dispute them — to my notice? Supposing I refuse you remuneration? '

Mills had noted the signs of agitation and anxiety. He felt that he was on safe ground. The blackmailer lives entirely on the want of courage in his victims.

'You will not, I hope, refuse me remuneration,' he said. 'I have not threatened you yet, because I feel sure you will be wise. I might, of course, subsequently threaten you.'

Again there was silence. Mr Taynton had picked up a quill pen, the same with which he had been writing before, for the nib was not yet dry.

'The law is rather severe on blackmailers,' he remarked.

'It is. Are you going to bring an action against me for blackmail? Will not that imply the re-opening of — of certain ledgers, which we agreed last night had better remain shut?'

Again there was silence. There was a completeness in this reasoning which rendered comment superfluous.

'How much do you want?' asked Mr Taynton.

Mills was not so foolish as to 'breathe a sigh of relief'. But he noted with satisfaction that there was no sign of fight in his adversary and partner.

'I want two thousand pounds,' he said, 'at once.'

'That is a large sum.'

'It is. If it were a small sum I should not trouble you.'

Mr Taynton again got up and strayed aimlessly about the room.

'I can't give it you today,' he said. 'I shall have to sell out some stock.'

'I am not unreasonable about a reasonable delay,' said Mills.

'You are going to town this afternoon?'

'Yes, I must. There is a good deal of work to be done. It will take me all tomorrow.'

'And you will be back the day after tomorrow?'

'Yes, I shall be back here that night, that is to say, I shall not get away from town till the afternoon. I should like your definite answer then, if it is not inconvenient. I could come and see you that night, the day after tomorrow — if you wished.'

Mr Taynton thought over this with his habitual deliberation.

'You will readily understand that all friendly relations between us are quite over,' he said. 'You have done a cruel and wicked thing, but I don't see how I can resist it. I should like, however, to have a little further talk about it, for which I have not time now.'

Mills rose.

'By all means,' he said. 'I do not suppose I shall be back here till nine in the evening. I have had no exercise lately, and I think very likely I shall get out of the train at Falmer, and walk over the downs.'

Mr Taynton's habitual courtesy came to his aid. He would have been polite to a thief or a murderer, if he met him socially.

'Those cool airs of the downs are very invigorating,' he said. 'I will not expect you therefore till half past nine that night. I shall dine at home, and be alone.'

'Thanks. I must be going. I shall only just catch my train to town.'

Mills nodded a curt gesture of farewell, and left the room, and when he had gone Mr Taynton sat down again in the chair by the table, and remained there some half hour. He knew well the soundness of his partner's reasoning; all he had said was fatally and abominably true. There was no way out of it. Yet to pay money to a blackmailer was, to the legal mind, a confession of guilt. Innocent people, unless they were abject fools, did not pay blackmail. They prosecuted the blackmailer. Yet here, too, Mills's simple reasoning held good. He could not prosecute the blackmailer, since he was not in the fortunate position of being innocent. But if you paid a blackmailer once, you were for ever in his power. Having once yielded, it was necessary to yield again. He must get some assurance that no further levy would take place. He must satisfy himself that he would be quit of all future danger from this quarter. Yet from whence was such assurance to come? He might have it a hundred times over in Godfrey Mills's handwriting, but he could never produce that as evidence, since again the charge of fraudulent employment of clients' money would be in the air. No doubt, of course, the blackmailer would be sentenced, but the cause of blackmail would necessarily be public. No, there was no way out.

Two thousand pounds, though! Frugally and simply as he lived, that was to him a dreadful sum, and represented the savings of at least eighteen months. This meant that there was for him another eighteen months of work, just when he hoped to see his retirement coming close to him. Mills demanded that he should work an extra year and a half, and out of those few years that in all human probability still remained to him in this pleasant world. Yet there was no way out!

Half an hour's meditation convinced him of this, and, as was his sensible plan, when a thing was inevitable, he never either fought against it nor wasted energy in regretting it. And he went slowly out of the office into which he had come so briskly an hour or two before. But his face expressed no sign of disquieting emotion; he nodded kindly to Timmins, and endorsed his desire to be allowed to come and see the grandson. If anything was on his mind, or if he was revolving some policy for the future, it did not seem to touch or sour that kindly, pleasant face.

Chapter IV

MR TAYNTON did not let these very unpleasant occurrences interfere with the usual and beneficent course of his life, but faced the crisis with that true bravery that not only meets a thing without flinching, but meets it with the higher courage of cheerfulness, serenity and ordinary behaviour. He spent the rest of the day in fact in his usual manner, enjoying his bathe before lunch, his hour of the paper and the quiet cigar afterward, his stroll over the springy turf of the downs, and he enjoyed also the couple of hours of work that brought him to dinner time. Then afterward he spent his evening, as was his weekly custom, at the club for young men which he had founded, where instead of being exposed to the evening lures of the sea front and the public house, they could spend (on payment of a really nominal subscription) a quieter and more innocent hour over chess, bagatelle and the illustrated papers, or if more energetically disposed, in the airy gymnasium adjoining the reading-room, where they could indulge in friendly rivalry with

boxing gloves or single-stick, or feed the appetites
of their growing muscles with dumb-bells and
elastic contrivances. Mr Taynton had spent a couple
of hours there, losing a game of chess to one
youthful adversary, but getting back his laurels over
bagatelle, and before he left, had arranged for a
geological expedition to visit, on the Whitsuntide
bank holiday next week, the curious raised beach
which protruded so remarkably from the range of
chalk downs some ten miles away.

On returning home, it is true he had deviated a
little from his usual habits, for instead of devoting
the half-hour before bed-time to the leisurely
perusal of the evening paper, he had merely given
it one glance, observing that copper was strong
and that Boston Copper in particular had risen
half a point, and had then sat till bed-time doing
nothing whatever, a habit to which he was not
generally addicted.

He was seated in his office next morning and was
in fact on the point of leaving for his bathe, for this
hot genial June was marching on its sunny way
uninterrupted by winds or rain, when Mr Timmins,
after discreetly tapping, entered, and closed the
door behind him.

'Mr Morris Assheton, sir, to see you,' he said. 'I
said I would find out if you were disengaged, and
could hardly restrain him from coming in with
me. The young gentleman seems very excited and
agitated. Hardly himself, sir.'

'Indeed, show him in,' said Mr Taynton.

A moment afterward the door burst open and

banged to again behind Morris. High colour flamed in his face, his black eyes sparkled with vivid dangerous light, and he had no salutation for his old friend.

I've come on a very unpleasant business,' he said, his voice not in control.

Mr Taynton got up. He had only had one moment of preparation and he thought, at any rate, that he knew for certain what this unpleasant business must be. Evidently Mills had given him away. For what reason he had done so he could not guess; after his experience of yesterday it might have been from pure devilry, or again he might have feared that in desperation, Taynton would take that extreme step of prosecuting him for blackmail. But, for that moment Taynton believed that Morris's agitation must be caused by this, and it says much for the iron of his nerve that he did not betray himself by a tremor.

'My dear Morris,' he said, 'I must ask you to pull yourself together. You are out of your own control. Sit down, please, and be silent for a minute. Then tell me calmly what is the matter.'

Morris sat down as he was told, but the calmness was not conspicuous.

'Calm?' he said. 'Would you be calm in my circumstances, do you think?'

'You have not yet told me what they are,' said Mr Taynton.

'I've just seen Madge Templeton,' he said. 'I met her privately by appointment. And she told me — she told me——'

Master of himself though he was, Mr Taynton had one moment of physical giddiness, so complete and sudden was the revulsion and reaction that took place in his brain. A moment before he had known, he thought, for certain that his own utter ruin was imminent. Now he knew that it was not that, and though he had made one wrong conjecture as to what the unpleasant business was, he did not think that his second guess was far astray.

'Take your time, Morris,' he said. 'And, my dear boy, try to calm yourself. You say I should not be calm in your circumstances. Perhaps I should not, but I should make an effort. Tell me everything slowly, omitting nothing.'

This speech, combined with the authoritative personality of Mr Taynton, had an extraordinary effect on Morris. He sat quiet a moment or two, then spoke.

'Yes, you are quite right,' he said, 'and after all I have only conjecture to go on yet, and I have been behaving as if it was proved truth. God! if it is proved to be true, though, I'll expose him, I'll — I'll horsewhip him, I'll murder him!'

Mr Taynton slapped the table with his open hand.

'Now, Morris, none of these wild words,' he said. 'I will not listen to you for a moment, if you do not control yourself.'

Once again, and this time more permanently, the man's authority asserted itself. Morris again sat silent for a time, then spoke evenly and quietly.

'Two nights ago you were dining with us,' he

said, 'and Madge was there. Do you remember my asking her if I might come to see them, and she said she and her mother would be out all day?'

'Yes; I remember perfectly,' said Mr Taynton.

'Well, yesterday afternoon I was motoring by the park, and I saw Madge sitting on the lawn. I stopped the motor and watched. She sat there for nearly an hour, and then Sir Richard came out of the house and they walked up and down the lawn together.'

'Ah, you must have been mistaken,' said Mr Taynton. 'I know the spot you mean on the road, where you can see the lawn, but it's half a mile off. It must have been some friend of hers perhaps staying in the house.'

Morris shook his head.

'I was not mistaken,' he said. 'For yesterday evening I got a note from her, saying she had posted it secretly, but that she must see me, though she was forbidden to do so, or to hold any communication with me.'

'Forbidden?' ejaculated Mr Taynton.

'Yes, forbidden. Well, this morning I went to the place she named, outside on the downs beyond the park gate and saw her. Somebody has been telling vile lies about me to her father. I think I know who it is.'

Mr Taynton held up his hand.

'Stop,' he said, 'let us have your conjecture afterward. Tell me first not what you guess, but what happened. Arrange it all in your mind, tell it me as connectedly as you can.'

Morris paused a moment.

'Well, I met Madge as I told you, and this was her story. Three days ago she and her father and mother were at lunch, and they had been talking in the most friendly way about me, and it was arranged to ask me to spend all yesterday with them. Madge, as you know, the next night was dining with us, and it was agreed that she should ask me verbally. After lunch she and her father went out riding, and when they returned they found that your partner Mills had come to call. He stayed for tea, and after tea had a talk alone with Sir Richard, while she and her mother sat out on the lawn. Soon after he had gone, Sir Richard sent for Lady Templeton, and it was nearly dressing-time when she left him again. She noticed at dinner that both her father and mother seemed very grave, and when Madge went up to bed, her mother said that perhaps they had better not ask me over, as there was some thought of their being away all day. Also if I suggested coming over, when Madge dined with us, she was to give that excuse. That was all she was told for the time being.'

Morris paused again.

'You are telling this very clearly and well, my dear boy,' said the lawyer, very gravely and kindly.

'It is so simple,' said he with a biting emphasis. 'Then next morning after breakfast her father sent for her. He told her that they had learned certain things about me which made them think it better not to see any more of me. What they were, she was not told, but, I was not, it appeared, the sort of person with whom they chose to associate. Now, before God, those things that they were told, whatever they were, were lies. I lead a straight and sober life.'

Mr Taynton was attending very closely.

'Thank God, Madge did not believe a word of it,' said Morris, his face suddenly flushing, 'and like a brick, and a true friend, she wrote at once to me, as I said, in order to tell me all this. We talked over, too, who it could have been who had said these vile things to her father. There was only one person who could. She had ridden with her father till tea-time. Then came your partner. Sir Richard saw nobody else; nobody else called that afternoon; no post came in.'

Mr Taynton had sprung up and was walking up and down the room in great agitation.

'I can't believe that,' he said. 'There must be some other explanation. Godfrey Mills say those things about you! It is incredible. My dear boy, until it is proved, you really must not let yourself believe that to be possible. You can't believe such wickedness against a man, one, too, whom I have known and trusted for years, on no evidence. There is no direct evidence yet. Let us leave that alone for the moment. What are you going to do now?'

'I came here to see him,' said Morris. 'But I am told he is away. So I thought it better to tell you.'

'Yes, quite right. And what else?'

'I have written to Sir Richard, demanding, in common justice, that he should see me, should tell me what he has heard against me, and who told him. I don't think he will refuse. I don't see how he can refuse. I have asked him to see me tomorrow afternoon.'

Mr Taynton mentally examined this in all its bearings. Apparently it satisfied him.

'You have acted wisely and providently,' he said. 'But I want to beg you, until you have definite information, to forbear from thinking that my dear Mills could conceivably have been the originator of these scandalous tales, tales which I know from my knowledge of you are impossible to be true. From what I know of him, however, it is impossible he could have said such things. I cannot believe him capable of a mean or deceitful action, and that he should be guilty of such unfathomable iniquity is simply out of the question. You must assume him innocent till his guilt is proved.'

'But who else could it have been?' cried Morris, his voice rising again.

'It could not have been he,' said Taynton firmly.

There was a long silence; then Morris rose.

'There is one thing more,' he said, 'which is the most important of all. This foul scandal about me, of course, I know will be cleared up, and I shall be competent to deal with the offender. But — but Madge and I said other things to each other. I told her what I told you, that I loved her. And she loves me.'

The sternness, the trouble, the anxiety all melted from Mr Taynton's face.

'Ah, my dear fellow, my dear fellow,' he said with outstretched hands. 'Thank you for telling me. I am delighted, overjoyed, and indeed, as you say, that is far more important than anything else. My dear Morris, and is not your mother charmed?'

Morris shook his head.

'I have not told her yet, and I shall not till this is cleared up. It is her birthday the day after tomorrow; perhaps I shall be able to tell her then.'

He rose.

'I must go,' he said. 'And I will do all I can to keep my mind off accusing him, until I know. But when I think of it, I see red.'

Mr Taynton patted his shoulder affectionately.

'I should have thought that you had got something to think about, which would make it easy for you to prevent your thoughts straying elsewhere,' he said.

'I shall need all the distractions I can get,' said Morris rather grimly.

Morris walked quickly back along the sea front toward Sussex Square, and remembered as he went that he had not yet bought any gift for his mother on her birthday. There was something, too, which she had casually said a day or two ago that she wanted, what was it? Ah, yes, a new blotting book for her writing-table in the drawing-room. The shop she habitually dealt at for such things, a branch of

Asprey's, was only a few yards farther on, and he turned in to make inquiries as to whether she had ordered it. It appeared that she had been in that very morning, but the parcel had not been sent yet. So Morris, taking the responsibility on himself, counterordered the plain red morocco book she had chosen, and chose another, with fine silver scrollwork at the corners. He ordered, too, that a silver lettered inscription should be put on it 'H. A. from M. A.' with the date, two days ahead, 'June 24th, 1905'. This he gave instructions should be sent to the house on the morning of June 24th, the day after tomorrow. He wished it to be sent so as to arrive with the early post on that morning.

The promise which Morris had made his old friend not to let his thoughts dwell on suspicion and conjecture as yet uncertain of foundation was one of those promises which are made in absolute good faith, but which in their very nature cannot be kept. The thought of the hideous treachery, the gratuitous falsehood, of which, in his mind, he felt convinced Godfrey Mills had been guilty was like blood soaking through a bandage. All that he could do was to continue putting on fresh bandages — that was all of his promise that he was able to fulfil, and in spite of the bandages the blood stained and soaked its way through. In the afternoon he took out the motor, but his joy in it for the time was dead, and it was only because in the sense of pace and swift movement he hoped to find a narcotic to thought, that he went out at all. But there was no narcotic there, nor even in the thought of this huge joy of love that had dawned on him was there forgetfulness for all else, joy and sorrow and love, were for the present separated from him by these hideous and libellous things that had been said about him. Until they were removed, until they passed into non-existence again, nothing had any significance for him. Everything was coloured with them; bitterness as of blood tinged everything. Hours, too, must pass before they could be removed; this long midsummer day had to draw to its end, night had to pass; the hour of early dawn, the long morning had to be numbered with the past before he could even learn who was responsible for this poisoned tale.

And when he learned, or rather when his conjecture was confirmed as to who it was (for his supposition was conjecture in the sense that it only wanted the actual seal of reality on it) what should he do next? Or rather what must he do next? He felt that when he knew absolutely for certain who had said this about him, a force of indignation and hatred, which at present he kept chained up, must infallibly break its chain, and become merely a wild beast let loose. He felt he would be no longer responsible for what he did, something had to happen; something more than mere apology or retraction of words. To lie and slander like that was a crime, an insult against human and divine justice. It would be nothing for the criminal to say he was sorry; he had to be punished. A man who did that was not fit to live; he was a man no longer, he was a biting, poisonous reptile, who for the sake of the community must be expunged. Yet human justice which hanged people for violent crimes committed under great provocation, dealt more lightly with this far more devilish thing, a crime committed coldly and calculatingly, that had planned not the mere death of his body, but the disgrace and death of his character. Godfrey Mills — he checked the word and added to himself 'if it was he' — had morally tried to kill him.

Morris, after his interview that morning with Mr Taynton, had lunched alone in Sussex Square, his mother having gone that day up to London for two nights. His plan had been to go up with her, but he had excused himself on the plea of business with his trustees, and she had gone alone. Directly after lunch he had taken the motor out, and had whirled along the coast road, past Rottingdean through Newhaven and Seaford, and ten miles farther until the suburbs of Eastbourne had begun. There he turned, his thoughts still running a mill-race in his head, and retracing his road had by now come back to within a mile of Brighton again. The sun gilded the smooth channel, the winds were still, the hot midsummer afternoon lay heavy on the land. Then he stopped the motor and got out, telling Martin to wait there.

He walked over the strip of velvety down grass to the edge of the white cliffs, and there sat down. The sea below him whispered and crawled, above the sun was the sole tenant of the sky, and east and west the down was empty of passengers. He, like his soul, was alone, and alone he had to think these things out.

Yes, this liar and slanderer, whoever he was, had tried to kill him. The attempt had been well-planned too, for the chances had been a thousand to one in favour of the murderer. But the one chance had turned up, Madge had loved him, and she had been brave, setting at defiance the order of her father, and had seen him secretly, and told him all the circumstances of this attack on him. But supposing she had been just a shade less brave, supposing her filial obedience had weighed an ounce heavier? Then he would never have known anything about it. The result would simply have been, as it was meant to be, that the Templetons were out when he called. There would have been a change of subject in their rooms when his name was mentioned, other people would have vaguely gathered that Mr Morris Assheton's name was not productive of animated conversation; their gatherings would have spread further, while he himself, ignorant of all cause, would have encountered cold shoulders.

Morris's hands clutched at the short down grass, tearing it up and scattering it. He was helpless, too, unless he took the law into his own hands. It would do no good, young as he was, he knew that, to bring any action for defamation of character, since the world only says, if a man justifies himself by the only legal means in his power, 'There must have been something in it, since it was said!' No legal remedy, no fines or even imprisonment, far less apology and retraction satisfied justice. There were only two courses open: one to regard the slander as a splash of mud thrown by some vile thing that sat in the gutter, and simply ignore it; the other to do something himself, to strike, to hit, with his bodily hands, whatever the result of his violence was.

He felt his shoulder-muscles rise and brace themselves at the thought, all the strength and violence of his young manhood, with its firm sinews and supple joints, told him that it was his willing and active servant and would do his pleasure. He wanted to smash the jaw bone that had formed these lies, and he wanted the world to know he had done so. Yet that was not enough, he wanted to throttle the throat from which the words had come; the man ought to be killed; it was right to kill him just as it was right to kill a poisonous snake that somehow disguised itself as a man, and was received into the houses of men.

Indeed, should Morris be told, as he felt sure he would be, who his slanderer and defamer was, that gentleman would be wise to keep out of his way with him in such a mood. There was danger and death abroad on this calm hot summer afternoon.

Chapter V

It was about four o'clock on the afternoon of the following day, and Mr Taynton was prolonging his hour of quietude after lunch, and encroaching thereby into the time he daily dedicated to exercise. It was but seldom that he broke into the routine of habits so long formed, and indeed the most violent rain or snow of winter, the most cutting easterly blasts of March, never, unless he had some definite bodily ailment, kept him indoors or deprived him of his brisk health-giving trudge over the downs or along the sea front. But occasionally when the weather was unusually hot, he granted himself the indulgence of sitting still instead of walking, and certainly today the least lenient judge might say that there were strong extenuating circumstances in his favour. For the heat of the past week had been piling itself up, like the heaped waters of flood, and this afternoon was intense in its heat, its stillness and sultriness. It had been sunless all day, and all day the blanket of clouds that beset the sky had been gathering themselves into blacker and

more ill-omened density. There would certainly be
a thunderstorm before morning, and the approach
of it made Mr Taynton feel that he really had
not the energy to walk. By and by perhaps he
might be tempted to go in quest of coolness along
the sea front, or perhaps later in the evening he
might, as he sometimes did, take a carriage up
on to the downs, and come gently home to a
late supper. He would have time for that today,
for according to arrangement his partner was to
drop in about half past nine that evening. If he
got back at nine, supposing he went at all, he
would have time to have some food before receiving
him.

He sat in a pleasant parqueted room looking out
into the small square garden at the back of his house
in Montpellier Road. Big awnings stretched from
the window over the broad gravel path outside,
and in spite of the excessive heat the room was full
of dim coolness. There was but little furniture in
it, and it presented the strongest possible contrast
to the appointments of his partner's flat with its
heavy decorations, its somewhat gross luxury. A
few water-colours hung on the white walls, a few
Persian rugs strewed the floor, a big bookcase with
china on the top filled one end of the room, his
writing-table, a half dozen of Chippendale chairs,
and the chintz-covered sofa where he now lay
practically completed the inventory of the room.
Three or four bronzes, a Narcissus, a fifteenth-
century Italian St Francis, and a couple of Greek
reproductions stood on the chimney-piece, but the

whole room breathed an atmosphere of aesthetic asceticism.

Since lunch Mr Taynton had glanced at the paper, and also looked up the trains from Lewes in order to assure himself that he need not expect his partner till half past nine, and since then, though his hands and his eyes had been idle, his mind had been very busy. Yet for all its business, he had not arrived at much. Morris, Godfrey Mills, and himself; he had placed these three figures in all sorts of positions in his mind, and yet every combination of them was somehow terrible and menacing. Try as he would he could not construct a peaceful or secure arrangement of them. In whatever way he grouped them there was danger.

The kitchen passage ran out at right angles to the room in which he sat, and formed one side of the garden. The windows in it were high up, so that it did not overlook the flowerbeds, and on this torrid afternoon they were all fully open. Suddenly from just inside came the fierce clanging peal of a bell, which made him start from his recumbent position. It was the front-door bell, as he knew, and as it continued ringing as if a maniac's grip was on the handle, he heard the steps of his servant running along the stone floor of the passage to see what imperative summons this was. Then, as the front door was opened, the bell ceased as suddenly as it had begun, and the moment afterward he heard Morris's voice shrill and commanding.

'But he has got to see me,' he cried. 'What's the use of you going to ask if he will?'

Mr Taynton went to the door of his room which opened into the hall.

'Come in, Morris,' he said.

Though it had been Morris's hand which had raised so uncontrolled a clamour, and his voice that just now had been so uncontrolled, there was no sign, when the door of Mr Taynton's room had closed behind them, that there was any excitement of any sort raging within him. He sat down at once in a chair opposite the window, and Mr Taynton saw that in spite of the heat of the day and the violence of that storm which he knew was yelling and screaming through his brain, his face was absolutely white. He sat with his hands on the arms of the Chippendale chair, and they too were quite still.

'I have seen Sir Richard,' said he, 'and I came back at once to see you. He has told me everything. Godfrey Mills has been lying about me and slandering me.'

Mr Taynton sat down heavily on the sofa.

'No, no; don't say it, don't say it,' he murmured. 'It can't be true, I can't believe it.'

'But it is true, and you have got to believe it. He suggested that you should go and talk it over with him. I will drive you up in the car, if you wish——'

Mr Taynton waved his hand with a negative gesture.

'No, no, not at once,' he cried. 'I must think it over. I must get used to this dreadful, this appalling shock. I am utterly distraught.'

Morris turned to him, and across his face for one moment there shot, swift as a lightning-flash, a quiver of rage so rabid that he looked scarcely human, but like some Greek presentment of the Furies or Revenge. Never, so thought his old friend, had he seen such glorious youthful beauty so instinct and inspired with hate. It was the demoniacal force of that which lent such splendour to it. But it passed in a second, and Morris still very pale, very quiet spoke to him.

'Where is he?' he asked. 'I must see him at once. It won't keep.'

Then he sprang up, his rage again mastering him.

'What shall I do it with?' he said. 'What shall I do it with?'

For the moment Mr Taynton forgot himself and his anxieties.

'Morris, you don't know what you are saying,' he cried. 'Thank God nobody but me heard you say that!'

Morris seemed not to be attending.

'Where is he?' he said again. 'Are you concealing him here? I have already been to your office, and he wasn't there, and to his flat, and he wasn't there.'

Thank God,' ejaculated the lawyer.

'By all means if you like. But I've got to see him, you know. Where is he?'

'He is away in town,' said Mr Taynton, 'but he will be back tonight. Now attend. Of course you must see him, I quite understand that. But you mustn't see him alone, while you are like this.'

'No, I don't want to,' said Morris. 'I should like other people to see what I've got to — to say to him — that, that partner of yours.'

'He has from this moment ceased to be my partner,' said Mr Taynton brokenly. 'I could never again sign what he has signed, or work with him, or — or — except once — see him again. He is coming here by appointment at half past nine. Suppose that we all meet here. We have both got to see him.'

Morris nodded and went toward the door. A sudden spasm of anxiety seemed to seize Mr Taynton.

'What are you going to do now?' he asked.

'I don't know. Drive to Falmer Park perhaps, and tell Sir Richard you cannot see him immediately. Will you see him tomorrow?'

'Yes, I will call tomorrow morning. Morris, promise me you will do nothing rash, nothing that will bring sorrow on all those who love you.'

'I shall bring a little sorrow on a man who hates me,' said he.

He went out, and Mr Taynton sat down again, his mouth compressed into hard lines, his forehead heavily frowning. He could not permanently prevent Morris from meeting Godfrey Mills, besides, it was his right to do so, yet how fraught with awful risks to himself that meeting would be! Morris might easily make a violent, even a murderous, assault on the man, but Mills was an expert boxer and wrestler, science would probably get the upper hand of blind rage. But how deadly a weapon Mills had in store against himself; he would certainly tell Morris that if one partner had slandered him the other, whom he so trusted and revered, had robbed him; he would say, too, that Taynton had been cognizant of, and had approved, his slanders. There was no end to the ruin that would certainly be brought about his head if they met. Mills's train, too, would have left London by now; there was no chance of stopping him. Then there was another danger he had not foreseen, and it was too late to stop that now. Morris was going again to Falmer Park, had indeed started, and that afternoon Godfrey Mills would get out of the train, as he had planned, at the station just below, and walk back over the downs to Brighton. What if they met there, alone?

For an hour perhaps Mr Taynton delved at these problems, and at the end even it did not seem as if he had solved them satisfactorily, for when he went out of his house, as he did at the end of this time to get a little breeze if such was obtainable, his face was still shadowed and overclouded. Overclouded too was the sky, and as he stepped out into the street from his garden-room the hot air struck him like a buffet; and in his troubled and apprehensive mood it felt as if some hot hand warned him by a blow not to venture out of his house. But the house, somehow, in the last hour had become terrible to him, any movement or action, even on a day like this, when only madmen and the English go abroad, was better than the nervous waiting in his darkened room. Dreadful forces, forces of ruin

and murder and disgrace, were abroad in the world
of men; the menace of the low black clouds and
stifling heat was more bearable. He wanted to get
away from his house, which was permeated and
soaked in association with the other two actors,
who, in company with himself, had surely some
tragedy for which the curtain was already rung up.
Some dreadful scene was already prepared for them;
the setting and stage were ready, the prompter, and
who was he? was in the box ready to tell them the
next line if any of them faltered. The prompter,
surely he was destiny, fate, the irresistible course
of events, with which no man can struggle, any
more than the actor can struggle with or alter the
lines that are set down for him. He may mumble
them, he may act dispiritedly and tamely, but he
has undertaken a certain part; he has to go through
with it.

Though it was a populous hour of the day, there
were but few people abroad when Mr Taynton
came out to the sea front; a few cabs stood by the
railings that bounded the broad asphalt path which
faced the sea, but the drivers of these, despairing
of fares, were for the most part dozing on the
boxes, or with a more set purpose were frankly
slumbering in the interior. The dismal little wooden
shelters that punctuated the parade were deserted,
the pier stretched an untenanted length of boards
over the still, lead-coloured sea, and it seemed as
if nature herself was waiting for some elemental
catastrophe.

And though the afternoon was of such hideous

and sultry heat, Mr Taynton, though he walked somewhat more briskly than his wont, was conscious of no genial heat that produced perspiration, and the natural reaction and cooling of the skin. Some internal excitement and fever of the brain cut off all external things; the loneliness, the want of correspondence that fever brings between external and internal conditions, was on him. At one moment, in spite of the heat, he shivered, at another he felt that an apoplexy must strike him.

For some half-hour he walked to and fro along the sea-wall, between the blackness of the sky and the lead-coloured water, and then his thoughts turned to the downs above this stricken place, where even in the sultriest days some breath of wind was always moving. Just opposite him, on the other side of the road, was the street that led steeply upward to the station. He went up it.

It was about half past seven o'clock that evening that the storm burst. A few huge drops of rain fell on the hot pavements, then the rain ceased again, and the big splashes dried, as if the stones had been blotting paper that sucked the moisture in. Then without other warning a streamer of fire split the steeple of St Agnes's Church, just opposite Mr Taynton's house, and the crash of thunder answered it more quickly than his servant had run to open the door to Morris's furious ringing of the bell. At that the sluices of heaven were opened, and heaven's artillery thundered its salvoes to the flare of the reckless storm. In the next half-hour

a dozen houses in Brighton were struck, while the
choked gutters overflowing on to the streets made
ravines and waterways down the roadways. Then
the thunder and lightning ceased, but the rain still
poured down relentlessly and windlessly, a flood
of perpendicular water.

Mr Taynton had gone out without umbrella,
and when he let himself in by his latchkey at his
own house-door about half past eight, it was no
wonder that he wrung out his coat and trousers
so that he should not soak his Persian rugs. But
from him, as from the charged skies, some tension
had passed; this tempest which had so cooled the
air and restored the equilibrium of its forces had
smoothed the frowning creases of his brow, and
when the servant hurried up at the sound of the
banged front-door, he found his master soaked
indeed, but serene.

'Yes, I got caught by the storm, Williams,' he said,
'and I am drenched. The lightning was terrific, was
it not? I will just change, and have a little supper;
some cold meat, anything that there is. Yes, you
might take my coat at once.'

He divested himself of this.

'And I expect Mr Morris this evening,' he said.
'He will probably have dined, but if not I am sure
Mrs Otter will toss up a hot dish for him. Oh,
yes, and Mr Mills will be here at half-past nine,
or even sooner, as I cannot think he will have
walked from Falmer as he intended. But whenever
he comes, I will see him. He has not been here
already?'

'No, sir,' said Williams. 'Will you have a hot bath, sir?'

'No, I will just change. How battered the poor garden will look tomorrow after this deluge.'

Mr Taynton changed his wet clothes and half an hour afterwards he sat down to his simple and excellent supper. Mrs Otter had provided an admirable vegetable soup for him, and some cold lamb with asparagus and endive salad. A macedoine of strawberries followed and a scoop of cheese. Simple as his fare was, it just suited Mr Taynton's tastes, and he was indulging himself with the rather rare luxury of a third glass of port when Williams entered again.

'Mr Assheton,' he said, and held the door open.

Morris came in; he was dressed in evening clothes with a dinner jacket, and gave no salutation to his host.

'He's not come yet?' he asked.

But his host sprang up.

'Dear boy,' he said, 'what a relief it is to see you. Ever since you left this afternoon I have had you on my mind. You will have a glass of port?'

Morris laughed, a curious jangling laugh.

'Oh yes, to drink his health,' he said.

He sat down with a jerk, and leaned his elbows on the table.

He'll want a lot of health to carry him through this, won't he?' he asked.

He drank his glass of port like water, and Mr Taynton instantly filled it up again for him.

'Ah, I remember you don't like port,' he said. 'What else can I offer you?'

'Oh, this will do very well,' said Morris. 'I am so thirsty.'

'You have dined?' asked his host quietly.

'No; I don't think I did. I wasn't hungry.'

The Cromwellian clock chimed a remnant half hour.

'Half past,' said Morris, filling his glass again. 'You expect him then, don't you?'

'Mills is not always very punctual,' said Mr Taynton.

For the next quarter of an hour the two sat with hardly the interchange of a word. From outside came the swift steady hiss of the rain on to the shrubs in the garden, and again the clock chimed. Morris who at first had sat very quiet had begun to fidget and stir in his chair; occasionally when he happened to notice it, he drank off the port with which Mr Taynton hospitably kept his glass supplied. Sometimes he relit a cigarette only to let it go out again. But when the clock struck he got up.

'I wonder what has happened,' he said. 'Can he have missed his train? What time ought he to have got in?'

'He was to have got to Falmer,' said Mr Taynton with a little emphasis on the last word, 'at a quarter to seven. He spoke of walking from there.'

Morris looked at him with a furtive sidelong glance.

'Why, I — I might have met him there,' he said. 'I went up there again after I left you to tell Sir Richard you would call tomorrow.'

'You saw nothing of him?' asked the lawyer.

'No, of course not. Otherwise— There was scarcely a soul on the road; the storm was coming up. But he would go by the downs, would he not?'

'The path over the downs doesn't branch off for a quarter of a mile below Falmer station,' said Mr Taynton.

The minutes ticked on till ten. Then Morris went to the door.

'I shall go round to his rooms to see if he is there,' he said.

'There is no need,' said his host, 'I will telephone.'

The instrument hung in a corner of the room, and with very little delay, Mills's servant was rung up. His master had not yet returned, but he had said that he should very likely be late.

'And he made an appointment with you for half past nine?' asked Morris again.

'Yes. I cannot think what has happened to detain him.'

Morris went quickly to the door again.

'I believe it is all a trick,' he said, 'and you don't want me to meet him. I believe he is in his rooms the whole time. I shall go and see.'

Before Mr Taynton could stop him he had opened the front-door and banged it behind him, and was off hatless and coatless through the pouring perpendicular rain.

Mr Taynton ran to the door, as if to stop him, but Morris was already halfway down the street, and he went upstairs to the drawing-room. Morris was altogether unlike himself; this discovery of Mills's treachery seemed to have changed his nature. Violent and quick he always was, but tonight he was suspicious, he seemed to distrust Mr Taynton himself. And, a thing which his host had never known him do before, he had drunk, in that half hour when they sat waiting, close on a bottle of port.

The evening paper lay ready cut for him in its accustomed place, but for some five minutes Mr Taynton did not appear to notice it, though evening papers, on the money-market page, might contain news so frightfully momentous to him. But something, this strangeness in Morris, no doubt, and his general anxiety and suspense as to how this dreadful knot could unravel itself, preoccupied him now, and even when he did take up the paper and turn to the reports of Stock Exchange dealings, he was conscious of no more than a sort of subaqueous thrill of satisfaction. For Boston Copper had gone up nearly a point since the closing price of last night.

It was not many minutes, however, before Morris returned with matted and streaming hair and drenched clothes.

'He has not come back,' he said. 'I went to his rooms and satisfied myself of that, though I think they thought I was mad. I searched them you understand; I insisted. I shall go round there again first thing tomorrow morning, and if he is not there, I shall go up to find him in town. I can't wait; I simply can't wait.'

Mr Taynton looked at him gravely, then nodded.

'No, I guess how you are feeling,' he said. 'I cannot understand what has happened to Mills; I hope nothing is wrong, And now, my dear boy, let me implore you to go straight home, get off your wet things and go to bed. You will pay heavily for your excitement, if you are not careful.'

'I'll get it out of him,' said Morris.

Chapter VI

MORRIS, as Mr Taynton had advised, though not
because he advised it, had gone straight home to
the house in Sussex Square, had stripped off his
dripping clothes, and then, since this was the line
of least resistance, had gone to bed. He did not feel
tired, and he longed with that aching longing of the
son for the mother, that Mrs Assheton had been
here, so that he could just be in her presence, and,
if he found himself unable to speak and tell her
all the hideous happenings of those last days, let
her presence bring a sort of healing to his tortured
mind. But though he was conscious of no tiredness,
he was tired to the point of exhaustion, and he
had hardly got into bed, when he fell fast asleep.
Outside, hushing him to rest, there sounded the
sibilant rain, and from the sea below ripples broke
gently and rhythmically on the pebbly beach. Nature,
too, it seemed, was exhausted by that convulsion
of the elements that had turned the evening into a
clamorous hell of fire and riot, and now from very
weariness she was weeping herself asleep.

It was not yet eleven when Morris had got home, and he slept dreamlessly with that recuperative sleep of youth for some six hours. Then, as within the secret economy of the brain the refreshment of slumber repaired the exhaustion of the day before, he began to dream with strange lurid distinctness, a sort of resurrection dream of which the events of the two days before supplied the bones and skeleton outline. As in all very vivid and dreadful dreams the whole vision was connected and coherent, there were no ludicrous and inconsequent interludes, none of those breakings of one thread and hurried seizures of another, which though one is dreaming very distinctly, supply some vague mental comfort, since even to the sleeper they are reminders that his experiences are not solid but mere phantasies woven by imperfect consciousness and incomplete control of thought. It was not thus that Morris dreamed; his dream was of the solid and sober texture of life.

He was driving in his motor, he thought, down the road from the house at Falmer Park, which through the gate of a disused lodge joins the main road, that leads from Falmer Station to Brighton. He had just heard from Sir Richard's own lips who it was who had slandered and blackened him, but, in his dream, he was conscious of no anger. The case had been referred to some higher power, some august court of supreme authority, which would certainly use its own instruments for its own vengeance. He felt he was concerned in the affair no longer; he was but a spectator of what would be. And, in obedience to some inward dictation, he drove his motor on to the grass behind the lodge, so that it was concealed from the road outside, and walked along the inside of the park-palings, which ran parallel with it.

The afternoon, it seemed, was very dark, though the atmosphere was extraordinarily clear, and after walking along the springy grass inside the railings for some three hundred yards, where was the southeastern corner of the park enclosure, he stopped at the angle and standing on tip-toe peered over them, for they were nearly six feet high, and looked into the road below. It ran straight as a billiard-cue just here, and was visible for a long distance, but at the corner, just outside the palings, the footpath over the downs to Brighton left the road, and struck upward. On the other side of the road ran the railway, and in this clear dark air, Morris could see with great distinctness Falmer Station some four hundred yards away, a a long stretch of the line on the other side of it.

As he looked he saw a puff of steam rise against the woods beyond the station, and before long a train, going Brightonward, clashed into the station. Only one passenger got out, and he came out of the station into the road. He was quite recognisable even at this distance. In his dream Morris felt that he expected to see him get out of the train, and walk along the road; the whole thing seemed pre-ordained. But he ceased tiptoeing to look over the paling; he could hear the passenger's steps when he came nearer.

He thought he waited quietly, squatting down on the mossy grass behind the paling. Something in his hands seemed angry, for his fingers kept tearing up the short turf, and the juice of the severed stems was red like blood. Then in the gathering darkness he heard the tip-tap of footsteps on the highway. But it never occurred to him that this passenger would continue on the highroad; he was certainly going over the downs to Brighton.

The air was quite windless, but at this moment Morris heard the boughs of the oak-tree immediately above him stir and shake, and looking up he saw Mr Taynton sitting in a fork of the tree. That, too, was perfectly natural; Mr Taynton was Mills's partner; he was there as a sort of umpire. He held a glass of port wine in one hand, and was sipping it in a leisurely manner, and when Morris looked up at him, he smiled at him, but put his finger to his lips, as if recommending silence. And as the steps on the road outside sounded close he turned a meaning glance in the direction of the road. From where he sat high in the tree, it was plain to Morris that he must command the sight of the road, and was, in his friendly manner, directing operations.

Suddenly the sound of the steps ceased, and Morris wondered for the moment whether Mills had stopped. But looking up again, he saw Mr Taynton's head twisted round to the right, still looking over the palings. But Morris found at once that the footsteps were noiseless, not because the walker had paused, but because they were inaudible on

the grass. He had left the road, as the dreamer felt
certain he would, and was going over the downs
to Brighton. At that Morris got up, and still inside
the park railings, followed in the direction he had
gone. Then for the first time in his dream, he felt
angry, and the anger grew to rage, and the rage to
quivering madness. Next moment he had vaulted
the fence, and sprang upon the walker from behind.
He dealt him blows with some hard instrument,
belabouring his head, while with his left hand he
throttled his throat so that he could not scream.
Only a few were necessary, for he knew that each
blow went home, since all the savage youthful
strength of shoulder and loose elbow directed them.
Then he withdrew his left hand from the throttled
throat of the victim who had ceased to struggle,
and like a log he fell back on to the grass, and
Morris for the first time looked on his face. It was
not Mills at all; it was Mr Taynton.

The terror plucked him from his sleep; for a
moment he wrestled and struggled to raise his
head from the pillow and loosen the clutch of the
night-hag who had suddenly seized him, and with
choking throat and streaming brow he sat up in
bed. Even then his dream was more real to him
than the sight of his own familiar room, more real
than the touch of sheet and blanket or the dew
of anguish which his own hand wiped from his
forehead and throat. Yet, what was his dream? Was
it merely some subconscious stringing together of
suggestions and desires and event vivified in sleep

to a coherent story (all but that recognition of Mr Taynton, which was nightmare pure and simple), or *had it happened*?

With waking, anyhow, the public life, the life that concerned other living folk as well as himself, became predominant again. He had certainly seen Sir Richard the day before, and Sir Richard had given him the name of the man who had slandered him. He had gone to meet that man, but he had not kept his appointment, nor had he come back to his flat in Brighton. So today he, Morris, was going to call there once more, and if he did not find him, was going to drive up to London, and seek him there.

But he had been effectually plucked from further sleep, sleep had been strangled, and he got out of bed and went to the window. Nature, in any case, had swept her trouble away, and the pure sweet morning was beginning to dawn in lines of yellow and fleeces of rosy cloud on the eastern horizon.

All that riot and hurly-burly of thunder, the bull's eye flashing of lightning, the perpendicular rain were things of the past, and this morning a sky of pale limpid blue, flecked only by the thinnest clouds, stretched from horizon to horizon. Below, the mirror of the sea seemed as deep and as placid as the sky above it, and the inimitable freshness of the dawn spoke of a world rejuvenated and renewed.

It was, by his watch, scarcely five; in an hour it would be reasonable to call at Mills's flat, and see if he had come by the midnight train. If not his motor could be round by soon after six, and he would be in town by eight, before Mills, if he had slept there, would be thinking of starting for Brighton. He was sure to catch him.

Morris had drawn up the blind, and through the open window came the cool breath of the morning ruffling his hair, and blowing his night-shirt close to his skin, and just for that moment, so exquisite was this feeling of renewal and cleanness in the hour of dawn, he thought with a sort of incredulous wonder of the red murderous hate which had possessed him the evening before. He seemed to have been literally beside himself with anger and his words, his thoughts, his actions had been controlled by a force and a possession which was outside himself. Also the dreadful reality of his dream still a little unnerved him, and though he was himself now and awake, he felt that he had been no less himself when he throttled the throat of that abhorred figure that walked up the noiseless path over the downs to Brighton, and with vehement and savage blows clubbed it down. And then the shock of finding it was his old friend whom he had done to death! That, it is true, was nightmare pure and simple, but all the rest was clad in sober, convincing garb of events that had really taken place. He could not at once separate his dream from reality, for indeed what had he done yesterday after he had learned who his traducer had been? He scarcely knew; all events and facts seemed colourless compared to the rage and mad lust for vengeance which had occupied his entire consciousness.

Thus, as he dressed, the thoughts and the rage of yesterday began to stir and move in his mind again. His hate and his desire that justice should be done, that satisfaction should be granted him, was still in his heart. But now they were not wild and flashing flames; they burned with a hard, cold, even light. They were already part of himself, integral pieces and features of his soul. And the calm beauty and peace of the morning ceased to touch him, he had a stern piece of business to put through before he could think of anything else.

It was not yet six when he arrived at the house in which was Mills's flat. A few housemaids were about, but the lift was not yet working, and he ran upstairs and rang at the bell. It was answered almost immediately, for Mills's servant supposed it must be his master arriving at this early hour, since no one else would come then, and he opened the door, half dressed, with coat and trousers only put over his night things.

'Is Mr Mills back yet?' asked Morris.

'No, sir.'

Morris turned to go, but then stopped, his mind still half-suspicious that he had been warned by his partner, and was lying *perdu*.

'I'll give you another ten shillings,' he said, 'if you'll let me come in and satisfy myself.'

The man hesitated.

'A sovereign,' said Morris.

He went back to Sussex Square after this, roused

Martin, ordering him to bring the motor round at once, and drank a cup of tea, for he would breakfast in town. His mother he expected would be back during the morning, and at the thought of her he remembered that this was June 24th, her birthday, and that his present to her would be arriving by the early post. He gave orders, therefore, that a packet for him from Asprey's was not to be unpacked, but given to her on her arrival with her letters. A quarter of an hour later he was off, leaving Martin behind, since there were various businesses in the town which he wanted him to attend to.

Mr Taynton, though an earlier riser than his partner, considered that half past nine was soon enough to begin the day, and punctually at that time he came downstairs to read, as his custom was, a few collects and some short piece of the Bible to his servants, before having his breakfast. That little ceremony over he walked for a few minutes in his garden while Williams brought in his toast and tea-urn, and observed that though the flowers would no doubt be all the better for the liberal watering of the day before, it was idle to deny that the rain had not considerably damaged them. But his attention was turned from these things to Williams who told him that breakfast was ready, and also brought him a telegram. It was from Morris, and had been sent off from the Sloane Square office an hour before.

Mills is not in town; they say he left
yesterday afternoon. Please inform me if
you know whether this is so, or if you
are keeping him from me. Am delayed by
break-down. Shall be back about five.—
MORRIS, Bachelors' Club.

Mr Taynton read this through twice, as is the
habit of most people with telegrams, and sent, of
course, the reply that all he knew was that his
partner intended to come back last night, since
he had made an appointment with him. Should
he arrive during the day he would telegraph. He
himself was keeping nothing from Morris, and had
not had any correspondence or communication
with his partner since he had left Brighton for
town three days before.

The telegram was a long one, but Mr Taynton
still sat with poised pen. Then he added, 'Pray do
nothing violent, I implore you.' And he signed it.

He sat rather unusually long over his breakfast
this morning, though he ate but little, and from
the cheerful smiling aspect of his face it would
seem that his thoughts were pleasant to him. He
was certainly glad that Morris had not yet come
across Mills, for he trusted that the lapse of a day
or two would speedily calm down the lad's perfectly
justifiable indignation. Besides, he was in love, and
his suit had prospered; surely there were pleasanter
things than revenge to occupy him. Then his face
grew grave a moment as he thought of Morris's

mad, murderous outburst of the evening before, but that gravity was shortlived, and he turned with a sense of pleasant expectation to see recorded again the activity and strength of Boston Coppers. But the reality was far beyond his expectations; copper had been strong all day, and in the street afterward there had been renewed buying from quarters which were usually well informed. Bostons had been much in request, and after hours they had had a further spurt, closing at £7 10s. Already in these three days he had cleared his option, and at present prices the shares showed a profit of a point. Mills would have to acknowledge that his perspicacity had been at fault, when he distrusted this last purchase.

He left his house at about half-past ten, and again immured himself in the birdcage lift that carried him up to his partner's fiat, where he inquired if he had yet returned. Learning he had not, he asked to be given pen and paper, to write a note for him, which was to be given to him on his arrival.

DEAR MILLS,

Mr Morris Assheton has learned that you have made grave accusations about him to Sir Richard Templeton, Bart. That you have done so appears to be beyond doubt, and it of course rests with you to substantiate them. I cannot of course at present believe that you could have done so without conclusive evidence; on the other hand I cannot believe that Mr

Assheton is of the character which you have given him.

I therefore refrain, as far as I am able, from drawing any conclusion till the matter is cleared up.

I may add that he deeply resents your conduct; his anger and indignation were terrible to see.

Sincerely yours,
EDWARD TAYNTON.

GODFREY MILLS, ESQ.

Mr Taynton read this through, and glanced round, as if to see whether the servants had left the room. Then he sat with closed eyes for a moment, and took an envelope, and swiftly addressed it. He smudged it, however, in blotting it, and so crumpled it up, threw it into the waste-paper basket. He then addressed a second one, and into this he inserted his letter, and got up.

The servant was waiting in the little hall outside.

'Please give this to Mr Mills when he arrives,' he said. 'You expected him last night, did you not?'

Mr Taynton found on arrival at his office that, in his partner's absence, there was a somewhat heavy day of work before him, and foresaw that he would be occupied all afternoon and indeed probably up to dinner time. But he was able to get out for an hour at half-past twelve, at which time, if the weather was hot, he generally indulged in a swim. But today there was a certain chill in the air after yesterday's storm, and instead of taking his dip, he walked along the sea front toward Sussex Square. For in his warm-hearted way, seeing that Morris was, as he had said, to tell his mother today about his happy and thoroughly suitable love affair, Mr Taynton proposed to give a little *partie carrée* on the earliest possible evening, at which the two young lovers, Mrs Assheton, and himself would form the table. He would learn from her what was the earliest night on which she and Morris were disengaged, and then write to that delightful girl whose affections dear Morris had captured.

But at the corner of the square, just as he was turning into it, there bowled swiftly out a victoria drawn by two horses; he recognised the equipage, he recognised also Mrs Assheton who was sitting in it. Her head, however, was turned the other way, and Mr Taynton's hand, already halfway up to his hat, was spared the trouble of journeying farther.

But he went on to the house, since his invitation could be easily conveyed by a note which he would scribble there, and was admitted by Martin. Mrs Assheton, however, was out, a fact which he learned with regret, but, if he might write a note to her, his walk would not be wasted. Accordingly he was shown up into the drawing-room, where on the writing-table was laid an open blotting book. Even in so small a detail as a blotting book the careful appointment of the house was evident, for the blotting paper was absolutely clean and white, a virgin field.

Mr Taynton took up a quill pen, thought over for a moment the wording of his note and then wrote rapidly. A single side of notepaper was sufficient; he blotted it on the pad, and read it through. But something in it, it must be supposed, did not satisfy him, for he crumpled it up. Ah, at last and for the first time there was a flaw in the appointment of the house, for there was no waste-paper basket by the table. At any rate one must suppose that Mr Taynton did not see it, for he put his rejected sheet into his pocket.

He took another sheet of paper, selecting from the various stationery that stood in the case a plain piece, rejecting that which was marked with the address of the house, wrote his own address at the head, and proceeded for the second time to write his note of invitation.

But first he changed the quill for his own stylograph, and wrote with that. This was soon written, and by the time he had read it through it was dry, and did not require to be blotted. He placed it in a plain envelope, directed it, and with it in his hand left the room, and went briskly downstairs.

Martin was standing in the hall.

'I want this given to Mrs Assheton when she comes in, Martin,' he said.

He looked round, as he had done once before when speaking to the boy.

'I left it at the door,' he said with quiet emphasis. 'Can you remember that? I left it. And I hope, Martin, that you have made a fresh start, and that I

need never be obliged to tell anybody what I know
about you. You will remember my instructions? I
left this at the door. Thank you. My hat? Yes, and
my stick.'

Mr Taynton went straight back to his office, and
though this morning there had seemed to him to
be a good deal of work to be got through, he found
that much of it could be delegated to his clerks.
So before leaving to go to his lunch, he called in
Mr Timmins.

'Mr Mills not been here all morning?' he asked.
'No? Well, Timmins, there is this packet which I
want him to look at, if he comes in before I am
back. I shall be here again by five, as there is an
hour's work for me to do before evening. Yes,
that is all, thanks. Please tell Mr Mills I shall come
back, as I said. How pleasant this freshness is after
the rain. The 'clear shining after rain'. Wonderful
words! Yes, Mr Timmins, you will find the verse in
the second book of Samuel and the twenty-third
chapter.'

Chapter VII

MR TAYNTON made but a short meal of lunch, and ate but sparingly, for he meant to take a good walk this afternoon, and it was not yet two o'clock when he came out of his house again, stick in hand. It was a large heavy stick that he carried, a veritable club, one that it would be easy to recognise amid a host of others, even as he had recognised it that morning in the rather populous umbrella-stand in the hall of Mrs Assheton's house. He had, it may be remembered, more office work to get through before evening, so he prepared to walk out as far as the limits of the time at his disposal would admit and take the train back. And since there could be nothing more pleasurable in the way of walking than locomotion over the springy grass of the downs, he took, as he had done a hundred times before, the road that led to Falmer. A hundred yards out of Brighton there was a stile by the roadside; from there a footpath, if it could be dignified by the name of path at all, led over the hills to a corner of Falmer Park. From there three or four hundred

yards of highway would bring him to the station.
He would be in good time to catch the 4.30 train
back, and would thus be at his office again for an
hour's work at five.

His walk was solitary and uneventful, but, to
one of so delicate and sensitive a mind, full of tiny
but memorable sights and sounds. Up on these
high lands there was a considerable breeze, and
Mr Taynton paused for a minute or two beside
a windmill that stood alone, in the expanse of
down, watching, with a sort of boyish wonder,
the huge flails swing down and aspire again in
the circles of their tireless toil. A little farther on
was a grass-grown tumulus of Saxon times, and
his mind was distracted from the present to those
early days when the unknown dead was committed
to this wind-swept tomb. Forests of pine no doubt
then grew around his resting place, it was beneath
the gloom and murmur of their sable foliage that
this dead chief was entrusted to the keeping of
the kindly earth. He passed, too, over the lines
of a Roman camp; once this sunny empty down
re-echoed to the clang of arms, the voices of the
living were mingled with the cries and groans of
the dying, for without doubt this stronghold of
Roman arms was not won, standing, as it did,
on the topmost commanding slope of the hills,
without slaughter. Yet today the peaceful clumps of
cistus and the trembling harebell blossomed on the
battlefield.

From this point the ground declined swiftly to the
main road. Straight in front of him were the palings

of Falmer Park, and the tenantless down with its long smooth curves was broken up into sudden hillocks and depressions. Dells and dingles, some green with bracken, others half full of water lay to right and left of the path, which, as it approached the corner of the park, was more strongly marked than when it lay over the big open spaces. It was somewhat slippery, too, after the torrent of yesterday, and Mr Taynton's stick saved him more than once from slipping. But before he got down to the point where the corner of the park abutted on the main road, he had leaned on it too heavily, and for all its seeming strength, it had broken in the middle. The two pieces were but luggage to him and just as he came to the road, he threw them away into a wooded hollow that adjoined the path. The stick had broken straight across; it was no use to think of having it mended.

He was out of the wind here, and since there was still some ten minutes to spare, he sat down on the grassy edge of the road to smoke a cigarette. The woods of the park basked in the fresh sunshine; three hundred yards away was Falmer Station, and beyond that the line was visible for a mile as it ran up the straight valley. Indeed he need hardly move till he saw the steam of his train on the limit of the horizon. That would be ample warning that it was time to go.

Then from far away, he heard the throbbing of a motor, which grew suddenly louder as it turned the corner of the road by the station. It seemed to him to be going very fast, and the huge cloud of dust behind it endorsed his impression. But almost immediately after passing this corner it began to slow down, and the cloud of dust behind it died away.

At the edge of the road where Mr Taynton sat, there were standing several thick bushes. He moved a little away from the road, and took up his seat again behind one of them. The car came very slowly on, and stopped just opposite him. On his right lay the hollow where he had thrown the useless halves of his stick, on his left was the corner of the Falmer Park railings. He had recognised the driver of the car, who was alone.

Morris got out when he had stopped the car, and then spoke aloud, though to himself.

'Yes, there's the corner,' he said, 'there's the path over the downs. There——'

Mr Taynton got up and came toward him.

'My dear fellow,' he said. 'I have walked out from Brighton on this divine afternoon, and was going to take the train back. But will you give me the pleasure of driving back with you instead?'

Morris looked at him a moment as if he hardly thought he was real.

'Why, of course,' he said.

Mr Taynton was all beams and smiles.

'And you have seen Mills?' he asked. 'You have been convinced that he was innocent of the terrible suspicion? Morris, my dear boy, what is the matter?'

Morris had looked at him for a moment with

incredulous eyes. Then he had sat down and covered his face with his hands.

'It's nothing,' he said at length. 'I felt rather faint. I shall be better in a minute. Of course I'll drive you back.'

He sat huddled up with hidden face for a moment or two. Mr Taynton said nothing, but only looked at him. Then the boy sat up.

'I'm all right,' he said, 'it was just a dream I had last night. No, I have not seen Mills; they tell me he left yesterday afternoon for Brighton. Shall we go?'

For some little distance they went in silence; then it seemed that Morris made an effort and spoke.

'Really, I got what they call "quite a turn" just now,' he said. 'I had a curiously vivid dream last night about that corner, and you suddenly appeared in my dream quite unexpectedly, as you did just now.'

'And what was this dream?' asked Mr Taynton, turning up his coat collar, for the wind of their movement blew rather shrilly on to his neck.

'Oh, nothing particular,' said Morris carelessly, 'the vividness was concerned with your appearance; that was what startled me.'

Then he fell back into the train of thought that had occupied him all the way down from London.

'I believe I was half-mad with rage last night,' he said at length, 'but this afternoon, I think I am beginning to be sane again. It's true Mills tried to injure me, but he didn't succeed. And as you said last night I have too deep and intense a cause of happiness to give my thoughts and energies to anything so futile as hatred or the desire for revenge. He is punished already. The fact of his having tried to injure me like that was his punishment. Anyhow, I am sick and tired of my anger.'

The lawyer did not speak for a moment, and when he did his voice was trembling.

'God bless you, my dear boy,' he said gently.

Morris devoted himself for some little time to the guiding of the car.

'And I want you also to leave it all alone,' he said after a while. 'I don't want you to dissolve your partnership with him, or whatever you call it. I suppose he will guess that you know all about it, so perhaps it would be best if you told him straight out that you do. And then you can, well, make a few well-chosen remarks you know, and drop the whole damned subject forever.'

Mr Taynton seemed much moved.

'I will try,' he said, 'since you ask it. But Morris, you are more generous than I am.'

Morris laughed, his usual boyish high spirits and simplicity were reasserting themselves again.

'Oh, that's all rot,' he said. 'It's only because it's so fearfully tiring to go on being angry. But I can't help wondering what has happened to the fellow. They told me at his flat in town that he went off with his luggage yesterday afternoon, and gave orders that all letters were to be sent to his Brighton address. You don't think there's anything wrong, do you?'

'My dear fellow, what could be wrong?' asked Mr Taynton. 'He had some business to do at Lewes on his way down, and I make no doubt he slept there, probably forgetting all about his appointment with me. I would wager you that we shall find he is in Brighton when we get in.'

'I'll take that,' said Morris. 'Half a crown.'

'No, no, my usual shilling, my usual shilling,' laughed the other.

Morris set Mr Taynton down at his office, and by way of settling their wager at once, waited at the door, while the other went upstairs to see if his partner was there. He had not, however, appeared there that day, and Mr Taynton sent a clerk down to Morris, to ask him to come up, and they would ring up Mr Mills's flat on the telephone.

This was done, and before many seconds had elapsed they were in communication. His valet was there, still waiting for his master's return, for he had not yet come back. It appeared that he was getting rather anxious, for Mr Taynton reassured him.

'There is not the slightest cause for any anxiety,' were his concluding words. 'I feel convinced he has merely been detained. Thanks, that's all. Please let me know as soon as he returns.'

He drew a shilling from his pocket, and handed it to Morris. But his face, in spite of his reassuring words, was a little troubled. You would have said that though he might not yet be anxious, he saw that there was some possibility of his being so, before very long. Yet he spoke gaily enough.

'And I made so sure I should win,' he said. 'I shall put it down to unexpected losses, not connected with business; eh, Mr Timmins? Or shall it be charity? It would never do to put down "Betting losses".'

But this was plainly a little forced, and Morris waited till Mr Timmins had gone out.

'And you really meant that?' he asked. 'You are really not anxious?'

'No, I am not anxious,' he said, 'but — but I shall be glad when he comes back. Is that inconsistent? I think perhaps it is. Well, let us say then that I am just a shade anxious. But I may add that I feel sure my anxiety is quite unnecessary. That defines it for you.'

Morris went straight home from here, and found that his mother had just returned from her afternoon drive. She had found the blotting book waiting for her when she came back that morning, and was delighted with the gift and the loving remembering thought that inspired it.

'But you shouldn't spend your money on me, my darling,' she said to Morris, 'though I just love the impulse that made you.'

'Oh, very well,' said Morris, kissing her, 'let's have the initials changed about then, and let it be M. A. from H. A.'

Then his voice grew grave.

'Mother dear, I've got another birthday present for you. I think — I think you will like it.'

She saw at once that he was speaking of no tangible material gift.

'Yes, dear?' she said.

'Madge and me,' said Morris. 'Just that.'

And Mrs Assheton did like this second present, and though it made her cry a little, her tears were the sweetest that can be shed.

Mother and son dined alone together, and since Morris had determined to forget, to put out of his mind the hideous injury that Mills had attempted to do him, he judged it to be more consistent with this resolve to tell his mother nothing about it, since to mention it to another, even to her, implied that he was not doing his best to bury what he determined should be dead to him. As usual, they played backgammon together, and it was not till Mrs Assheton rose to go to bed that she remembered Mr Taynton's note, asking her and Morris to dine with him on their earliest unoccupied day. This, as is the way in the country, happened to be the next evening, and since the last post had already gone out, she asked Morris if Martin might take the note round for her tonight, since it ought to have been answered before.

That, of course, was easily done, and Morris told his servant to call also at the house where Mr Mills's flat was situated, and ask the porter if he had come home. The note dispatched his mother went to bed, and Morris went down to the billiard room to practise spot-strokes, a form of hazard at which he was singularly inefficient, and wait for news. Little as he knew Mills, and little cause as he had for liking him, he too, like Mr Taynton, felt vaguely anxious and perturbed, since 'disappearances' are necessarily hedged about with mystery and wondering. His own anger and hatred, too, like mists drawn up and dispersed by the sun of love that had dawned on him, had altogether vanished; the attempt against him had, as it turned out, been so futile, and he genuinely wished to have some assurance of the safety of the man, the thought of whom had so blackened his soul only twenty-four hours ago.

His errands took Martin the best part of an hour, and he returned with two notes, one for Mrs Assheton, the other for Morris. He had been also to the flat and inquired, but there was no news of the missing man.

Morris opened his note, which was from Mr Taynton.

DEAR MORRIS,

I am delighted that your mother and you can dine tomorrow, and I am telegraphing first thing in the morning to see if Miss Madge will make our fourth. I feel sure that when she knows what my little party is, she will come.

I have been twice round to see if my partner has returned, and find no news of him. It is idle to deny that I am getting anxious, as I cannot conceive what has happened. Should he not be back by tomorrow morning, I shall put the matter into the hands of the police. I trust that my anxieties are unfounded, but the matter is beginning to look strange.

Affectionately yours,
EDWARD TAYNTON.

There is nothing so infectious as anxiety, and it can be conveyed by look or word or letter, and requires no period of incubation. And Morris began to be really anxious also, with a vague disquietude at the sense of there being something wrong.

Chapter VIII

MR TAYNTON, according to the intention he had expressed, sent round early next morning (the day of the week being Saturday) to his partner's flat, and finding that he was not there, and that no word of any kind had been received from him, went, as he felt himself now bound to do, to the police office, stated what had brought him there, and gave them all information which it was in his power to give.

It was brief enough; his partner had gone up to town on Tuesday last, and, had he followed his plans, should have returned to Brighton by Thursday evening, since he had made an appointment to come to Mr Taynton's house at nine thirty that night. It had been ascertained too, by — Mr Taynton hesitated a moment — by Mr Morris Assheton in London, that he had left his flat in St James's Court on Thursday afternoon, to go, presumably, to catch the train back to Brighton. He had also left orders that all letters should be forwarded to him at his Brighton address.

Superintendent Figgis, to whom Mr Taynton made his statement, was in manner slow, stout, and bored, and looked in every way utterly unfitted to find clues to the least mysterious occurences, unearth crime or run down the criminal. He seemed quite incapable of running down anything, and Mr Taynton had to repeat everything he said in order to be sure that Mr Figgis got his notes, which he made in a large round hand, with laborious distinctness, correctly written. Having finished them the Superintendent stared at them mournfully for a little while, and asked Mr Taynton if he had anything more to add.

'I think that is all,' said the lawyer. 'Ah, one moment. Mr Mills expressed to me the intention of perhaps getting out at Falmer and walking over the downs to Brighton. But Thursday was the evening on which we had that terrible thunderstorm. I should think it very unlikely that he would have left the train.'

Superintendent Figgis appeared to be trying to recollect something.

'Was there a thunderstorm on Thursday?' he asked.

'The most severe I ever remember,' said Mr Taynton.

'It had slipped my memory,' said this incompetent agent of justice.

But a little thought enabled him to ask a question that bore on the case.

'He travelled then by Lewes and not by the direct route?'

'Presumably. He had a season ticket via Lewes, since our business often took him there. Had he intended to travel by Hayward's Heath,' said Mr Taynton rather laboriously, as if explaining something to a child, 'he could not have intended to get out at Falmer.'

Mr Figgis had to think over this, which he did with his mouth open.

'Seeing that the Hayward's Heath line does not pass Falmer,' he suggested.

Mr Taynton drew a sheet of paper toward him and kindly made a rough sketch-map of railway lines.

'And his season ticket went by the Lewes line,' he explained.

Superintendent Figgis appeared to understand this after a while. Then he sighed heavily, and changed the subject with rather disconcerting abruptness.

'From my notes I understand that Mr Morris Assheton ascertained that the missing individual had left his flat in London on Thursday afternoon,' he said.

'Yes, Mr Assheton is a client of ours, and he wished to see my partner on a business matter. In fact, when Mr Mills was found not to have returned on Thursday evening, he went up to London next day to see him, since we both supposed he had been detained there.'

Mr Figgis looked once more mournfully at his notes, altered a palpably mistaken 'Wednesday' into Thursday, and got up.

'The matter shall be gone into,' he said.

Mr Taynton went straight from here to his office, and for a couple of hours devoted himself to the business of his firm, giving it his whole attention and working perhaps with more speed than it was usually his to command. Saturday of course was a half-holiday, and it was naturally his desire to get cleared off everything that would otherwise interrupt the well-earned repose and security from business affairs which was to him the proper atmosphere of the seventh, or as he called it, the first day. This interview with the accredited representative of the law also had removed a certain weight from his mind. He had placed the matter of his partner's disappearance in official hands, he had done all he could do to clear up his absence, and, in case — but here he pulled himself up; it was at present most premature even to look at the possibility of crime having been committed.

Mr Taynton was in no way a vain man, nor was it his habit ever to review his own conduct, with the object of contrasting it favourably with what others might have done under the circumstances. Yet he could not help being aware that others less kindly than he would have shrugged sarcastic shoulders and said, 'Probably another blackmailing errand has detained him.' For, indeed, Mills had painted himself in very ugly colours in his last interview with him; that horrid hint of blackmail, which still, so to speak, held good, had cast a new light on him. But now Taynton was conscious of

no grudge against him; he did not say, 'He can look
after himself.' He was anxious about his continued
absence, and had taken the extreme step of calling
in the aid of the police, the national guardian of
personal safety.

He got away from his office about half past
twelve and in preparation for the little dinner
festival of this evening, for Miss Templeton had
sent her joyful telegraphic acceptance, went to
several shops to order some few little delicacies
to grace his plain bachelor table. An ice-pudding,
for instance, was outside the orbit, so he feared,
of his plain though excellent cook, and two little
dishes of chocolates and sweets, since he was at
the confectioner's, would be appropriate to the
taste of his lady guests. Again a floral decoration
of the table was indicated, and since the storm of
Thursday, there was nothing in his garden worthy
of the occasion; thus a visit to the florist's resulted
in an order for smilax and roses.

He got home, however, at his usual luncheon
hour to find a telegram waiting for him on the
Hepplewhite table in the hall. There had been a
continued buying of copper shares, and the feature
was a sensational rise in Bostons, which during the
morning had gone up a clear point.

Mr Taynton had no need to make calculations;
he knew, as a man knows the multiplication table
of two, what every fraction of a rise in Bostons
meant to him, and this, provided only he had
time to sell at once, meant the complete recovery

of the losses he had suffered. With those active markets it was still easily possible, though it was Saturday, to effect his sale, since there was sure to be long continued business in the Street and he had but to be able to exercise his option at that price, to be quit of that dreadful incubus of anxiety which for the last two years had been a millstone round his neck that had grown mushroom like. The telephone to town, of course, was far the quickest mode of communication, and having given his order he waited ten minutes till the tube babbled and croaked to him again.

There is a saying that things are 'too good to be true,' but when Mr Taynton sat down to his lunch that day, he felt that the converse of the proverb was the correcter epigram. Things could be so good that they must be true, and here, still ringing in his ears was one of them — Morris — it was thus he phrased it to himself — was 'paid off,' or, in more business-like language, the fortune of which Mr Taynton was trustee was intact again, and, like a tit-bit for a good child, there was an additional five or six hundred pounds for him who had managed the trust so well. Mr Taynton could not help feeling somehow that he deserved it; he had increased Morris's fortune since he had charge of it by £10,000. And what a lesson, too, he had had, so gently and painlessly taught him! No one knew better than he how grievously wrong he had got, in gambling with trust money. Yet now it had come right: he had repaired the original wrong; on Monday he would reinvest this

capital in those holdings which he had sold, and
Morris's £40,000 (so largely the result of careful
and judicious investment) would certainly stand
the scrutiny of any who could possibly have any
cause to examine his ledgers. Indeed there would be
nothing to see. Two years ago Mr Morris Assheton's
fortune was invested in certain railway debentures
and Government stock. It would in a few days' time
be invested there again, precisely as it had been.
Mr Taynton had not been dealing in gilt-edged
securities lately, and could not absolutely trust his
memory, but he rather thought that the repurchase
could be made at a somewhat smaller sum than had
been realised by their various sales dating from two
years ago. In that case there was a little more *sub
rosa* reward for this well-inspired justice, weighed
but featherwise against the overwhelming relief of
the knowledge he could make wrong things right
again, repair his, yes, his scoundrelism.

How futile, too, now, was Mills's threatened
blackmail! Mills might, if he chose, proclaim on
any convenient housetop, that his partner had
gambled with Morris's £40,000 that according to the
ledgers was invested in certain railway debentures
and other gilt-edged securities. In a few days, any
scrutiny might be made of the securities lodged
at the County Bank, and assuredly among them
would be found those debentures, those gilt-
edged securities exactly as they appeared in the
ledgers. Yet Mr Taynton, so kindly is the nature
of happiness, contemplated no revengeful step on
his partner; he searched his heart and found that

no trace of rancour against poor Mills was hoarded there.

Whether happiness makes us good, is a question not yet decided, but it is quite certain that happiness makes us forget that we have been bad, and it seemed to Mr Taynton, as he sat in his cool dining-room, and ate his lunch with a more vivid appetite than had been his for many months, it seemed that the man who had gambled with his client's money was no longer himself; it was a perfectly different person who had done that. It was a different man, too, who, so few days ago had connived at and applauded the sorry trick which Mills had tried to play on Morris, when (so futilely, it is true) he had slandered him to Sir Richard. Now he felt that he — this man that today sat here — was incapable of such meannesses. And, thank God, it was never too late; from today he would lead the honourable, upright existence which the world (apart from his partner) had always credited him with leading.

He basked in the full sunshine of these happy and comfortable thoughts, and even as the sun of midsummer lingered long on the sea and hills, so for hours this inward sunshine warmed and cheered him. Nor was it till he saw by his watch that he must return from the long pleasant ramble on which he had started as soon as lunch was over, that a cloud filmy and thin at first began to come across the face of the sun. Once and again those genial beams dispersed it, but soon it seemed as if the vapours were getting the upper hand. A thought, in fact, had crossed Mr Taynton's mind that quite distinctly dimmed his happiness. But a little reflection told him that a very simple step on his part would put that right again, and he walked home rather more quickly than he had set out, since he had this little bit of business to do before dinner.

He went — this was only natural — to the house where Mr Mills's flat was situated, and inquired of the porter whether his partner had yet returned. But the same answer as before was given him, and, saying that he had need of a document that Mills had taken home with him three days before, he went up in the lift, and rang the bell of the flat. But it was not his servant who opened it, but sad Superintendent Figgis.

For some reason this was rather a shock to Mr Taynton; to expect one face and see another is always (though ever so slightly) upsetting, but he instantly recovered himself and explained his errand.

'My partner took home with him on Tuesday a paper, which is concerned with my business,' he said. 'Would you kindly let me look round for it?'

Mr Figgis weighed this request.

'Nothing must be removed from the rooms,' he said, 'till we have finished our search.'

'Search for what?' asked Mr Taynton.

'Any possible clue as to the reason of Mr Mills's disappearance. But in ten minutes we shall have done, if you care to wait.'

'I don't want to remove anything,' said the lawyer. 'I merely want to consult——'

At the moment another man in plain clothes came out of the sitting-room. He carried in his hand two or three letters, and a few scraps of crumpled paper. There was an envelope or two among them.

'We have finished, sir,' he said to the Superintendent.

Mr Figgis turned to the lawyer, who was looking rather fixedly at what the other man had in his hand.

'My document may be among those,' he said.

Mr Figgis handed them to him. There were two envelopes, both addressed to the missing man, one bearing his name only, some small torn-up scraps of paper, and three or four private letters.

'Is it among these?' he asked.

Mr Taynton turned them over.

'No,' he said, 'it was — it was a large, yes, a large blue paper, official looking.'

'No such thing in the flat, sir,' said the second man.

'Very annoying,' said the lawyer.

An idea seemed slowly to strike Mr Figgis.

'He may have taken it to London with him,' he said. 'But will you not look round?'

Mr Taynton did so. He also looked in the waste-paper basket, but it was empty.

So he went back to make ready to receive his guests, for the little party. But it had got dark; this 'document', whatever it was, appeared to trouble

him. The simple step he had contemplated had not
led him in quite the right direction.

The Superintendent with his colleague went back
into the sitting-room on the lawyer's departure,
and Mr Figgis took from his pocket most of his
notes.

'I went to the station, Wilkinson,' he said,
'and in the lost luggage office I found Mr Mills's
bag. It had arrived on Thursday evening. But it
seems pretty certain that its owner did not arrive
with it.'

'Looks as if he did get out at Falmer,' said
Wilkinson.

Figgis took a long time to consider this.

'It is possible,' he said. 'It is also possible that
he put his luggage into the train in London, and
subsequently missed the train himself.'

Then together they went through the papers
that might conceivably help them. There was a
torn-up letter found in his bedroom fireplace,
and the crumpled-up envelope that belonged to
it. They patiently pieced this together, but found
nothing of value. The other letters referred only to
his engagements in London, none of which were
later than Thursday morning. There remained one
crumpled-up envelope (also from the paper-basket)
but no letter that in any way corresponded with
it. It was addressed in a rather sprawling, eager,
boyish hand.

'No letter of any sort to correspond?' asked Figgis
for the second time.

'No.'

'I think for the present we will keep it,' said he.

The little party at Mr Taynton's was gay to the point of foolishness, and of them all none was more light-hearted than the host. Morris had asked him in an undertone, on arrival, whether any more had been heard, and learning there was still no news, had dismissed the subject altogether, The sunshine of the day, too, had come back to the lawyer; his usual cheerful serenity was touched with a sort of sympathetic boisterousness at the huge spirits of the young couple and it was to be recorded that after dinner they played musical chairs and blind-man's buff, with infinite laughter. Never was an elderly solicitor so spontaneously gay; indeed before long it was he who reinfected the others with merriment. But as always, after abandonment to laughter a little reaction followed, and when they went upstairs from his sitting-room where they had been so uproarious, so that it might be made tidy again before Sunday, and sat in the drawing-room overlooking the street, there did come this little reaction. But it was already eleven, and soon Mrs Assheton rose to go.

The night was hot, and Morris was sitting to cool himself by the open window, leaning his head out to catch the breeze. The street was very empty and quiet, and his motor, in which as a great concession his mother had consented to be carried, on the promise of his going slow, had already come for them. Then down at the seaward end of the street he heard street-cries, as if some sudden news had come in that sent the vendors of the evening papers out to reap a second harvest that night. He could not, however, catch what it was, and they all went downstairs together.

Madge was going home with them, for she was stopping over the Sunday with Mrs Assheton, and the two ladies had already got into the car, while Morris was still standing on the pavement with his host.

Then suddenly a newsboy, with a sheaf of papers still hot from the press, came running from the corner of the street just above them, and as he ran he shouted out the news which was already making little groups of people collect and gather in the streets.

Mr Taynton turned quickly as the words became audible, seized a paper from the boy, giving him the first coin that he found, and ran back into the hall of his house, Morris with him, to beneath the electric light that burned there. The shrill voice of the boy still shouting the news of murder got gradually less loud as he went further down the street.

They read the short paragraph together, and then looked at each other with mute horror in their eyes.

Chapter IX

THE inquest was held at Falmer on the Monday following, when the body was formally identified by Mr Taynton and Mills's servant, and they both had to give evidence as regards what they knew of the movements of the deceased. This, as a matter of fact, Mr Taynton had already given to Figgis, and in his examination now he repeated with absolute exactitude what he had said before including again the fact that Morris had gone up to town on Friday morning to try to find him there. On this occasion, however, a few further questions were put to him, eliciting the fact that the business on which Morris wanted to see him was known to Mr Taynton but could not be by him repeated since it dealt with confidential transactions between the firm of solicitors and their client. The business was, yes, of the nature of a dispute, but Mr Taynton regarded it as certain that some amicable arrangement would have been come to, had the interview taken place. As it had not, however, since Morris had not found him at his flat in town, he could not speak for certain on this subject. The dispute concerned an action of his partner's, made independently of him. Had he been consulted he would have strongly disapproved of it.

The body, as was made public now, had been discovered by accident, though, as has been seen, the probability of Mills having got out at Falmer had been arrived at by the police, and Figgis immediately after his interview with Mr Taynton on the Saturday evening had started for Falmer to make inquiries there, and had arrived there within a few minutes of the discovery of the body. A carpenter of that village had strolled out about eight o'clock that night with his two children while supper was being got ready, and had gone a piece of the way up the path over the downs, which left the road at the corner of Falmer Park. The children were running and playing about, hiding and seeking each other in the bracken-filled hollows, and among the trees, when one of them screamed suddenly, and a moment afterward they both came running to their father, saying that they had come upon a man in one of these copses, lying on his face, and they were frightened. He had gone to see what this terrifying person was, and had found the body. He went straight back to the village without touching anything, for it was clear both from what he saw and from the crowd of buzzing flies that the man was dead, and gave information to the police. Then within a few minutes from that, Mr Figgis had arrived from Brighton, to find that it was superfluous to look any further or inquire any more concerning the whereabouts of the missing man. All that was mortal of him was here, the head covered with a cloth, and bits of the fresh summer growth of fern and frond sticking to his clothing.

After the identification of the body came evidence medical and otherwise that seemed to show beyond doubt the time and manner of his death and the possible motive of the murderer. The base of the skull was smashed in, evidently by some violent blow dealt from behind with a blunt heavy instrument of some sort, and death had probably been instantaneous. In one of the pockets was a first edition of an evening paper published in London on Thursday last, which fixed the earliest possible time at which the murder had been committed, while in the opinion of the doctor who examined the body late on Saturday night, the man had been dead not less than forty-eight hours. In spite of the very heavy rain which had fallen on Thursday night, there were traces of a pool of blood about midway between the clump of bracken where the body was found, and the path over the downs leading from Falmer to Brighton. This, taken in conjunction with the information already given by Mr Taynton, made it practically certain that the deceased had left London on the Thursday as he had intended to do, and had got out of the train at Falmer, also according to his expressed intention, to walk to Brighton. It would again have been most improbable that he would have started on his walk had the storm already

begun. But the train by which his bag was conveyed
to Brighton arrived at Falmer at half past six, the
storm did not burst till an hour afterward. Finally,
with regard to possible motive, the murdered man's
watch was missing; his pockets also were empty of
coin.

This concluded the evidence, and the verdict was
brought in without the jury leaving the court, and
'wilful murder by person or persons unknown'
was recorded.

Mr Taynton, as was indeed to be expected,
had been much affected during the giving of his
evidence, and when the inquest was over, he
returned to Brighton feeling terribly upset by this
sudden tragedy, which had crashed without warning
into his life. It had been so swift and terrible;
without sign or preparation this man, whom he
had known so long, had been hurled from life and
all its vigour into death. And how utterly now Mr
Taynton forgave him for that base attack that he
had made on him, so few days ago; how utterly,
too, he felt sure Morris had forgiven him for what
was perhaps even harder to forgive. And if they
could forgive trespasses like these, they who were of
human passion and resentments, surely the reader
of all hearts would forgive. That moment of agony
short though it might have been in actual duration,
when the murderous weapon split through the bone
and scattered the brain, surely brought punishment
and therefore atonement for the frailties of a lifetime.

Mr Taynton, on his arrival back at Brighton that afternoon, devoted a couple of solitary hours to such thoughts as these, and others to which this tragedy naturally gave rise and then with a supreme effort of will he determined to think no more on the subject. It was inevitable that his mind should again and again perhaps for weeks and months to come fall back on these dreadful events, but his will was set on not permitting himself to dwell on them. So, though it was already late in the afternoon, he set forth again from his house about tea-time, to spend a couple of hours at the office. He had sent word to Mr Timmins that he would probably come in, and begin to get through the arrears caused by his unavoidable absence that morning, and he found his head clerk waiting for him. A few words were of course appropriate, and they were admirably chosen.

'You have seen the result of the inquest, no doubt, Mr Timmins,' he said, 'and yet one hardly knows whether one wishes the murderer to be brought to justice. What good does that do, now our friend is dead? So mean and petty a motive too; just for a watch and a few sovereigns. It was money bought at a terrible price, was it not? Poor soul, poor soul; yes, I say that of the murderer. Well, well, we must turn our faces forward, Mr Timmins; it is no use dwelling on the dreadful irremediable past. The morning's post? Is that it?'

Mr Timmins ventured sympathy.

'You look terribly worn out, sir,' he said. 'Wouldn't it be wiser to leave it till tomorrow? A

good night's rest, you know, sir, if you'll excuse
my mentioning it.'

'No, no, Mr Timmins, we must get to work again,
we must get to work.'

Nature, inspired by the spirit and instinct of life,
is wonderfully recuperative. Whether earthquake or
famine, fire or pestilence has blotted out a thousand
lives, those who are left, like ants when their house
is disturbed, waste but little time after the damage
has been done in vain lamentations, but, slaves to
the force of life, begin almost instantly to rebuild
and reconstruct. And what is true of the community
is true also of the individual, and thus in three
days from this dreadful morning of the inquest,
Mr Taynton, after attending the funeral of the
murdered man, was very actively employed, since
the branch of the firm in London, deprived of its
head, required supervision from him. Others also,
who had been brought near to the tragedy, were
occupied again, and of these Morris in particular
was a fair example of the spirit of the Life-force. His
effort, no doubt, was in a way easier than that made
by Mr Taynton, for to be twenty-two years old and
in love should be occupation sufficient. But he, too,
had his bad hours, when the past rose phantom-
like about him, and he recalled that evening when
his rage had driven him nearly mad with passion
against his traducer. And by an awful coincidence,
his madness had been contemporaneous with the
slanderer's death. He must, in fact, have been within
a few hundred yards of the place at the time the

murder was committed, for he had gone back to
Falmer Park that day, with the message that Mr
Taynton would call on the morrow, and had left
the place not half an hour before the breaking of
the storm. He had driven by the corner of the Park,
where the path over the downs left the main road
and within a few hundred yards of him at that
moment, had been, dead or alive, the man who
had so vilely slandered him. Supposing — it might
so easily have happened — they had met on the
road. What would he have done? Would he have
been able to pass him and not wreaked his rage
on him? He hardly dared to think of that. But,
life and love were his, and that which might have
been was soon dreamlike in comparison of these.
Indeed, that dreadful dream which he had had the
night after the murder had been committed was no
less real than it. The past was all of this texture,
and mist-like, it was evaporated in the beams of
the day that was his.

Now Brighton is a populous place, and a sunny
one, and many people lounge there in the sun all
day. But for the next three or four days a few of
these loungers lounged somewhat systematically.
One lounged in Sussex Square, another lounged in
Montpellier Road, one or two others who apparently
enjoyed this fresh air but did not care about the town
itself, usually went to the station after breakfast,
and spent the day in rambling agreeably about the
downs. They also frequented the pleasant little
village of Falmer, gossiping freely with its rural
inhabitants. Often footmen or gardeners from the

Park came down to the village, and acquaintances
were easily ripened in the ale-house. Otherwise
there was not much incident in the village;
sometimes a motor drove by, and one, after an
illegally fast progress along the road, very often
turned in at the park gates. But no prosecution
followed; it was clear they were not agents of
the police. Mr Figgis, also, frequently came out
from Brighton, and went strolling about too, very
slowly and sadly. He often wandered in the little
copses that bordered the path over the downs to
Brighton, especially near the place where it joined
the main road a few hundred yards below Falmer
station. Then came a morning when neither he nor
any of the other chance visitors to Falmer were
seen there any more. But the evening before Mr
Figgis carried back with him to the train a long
thin package wrapped in brown paper. But on the
morning when these strangers were seen no more
at Falmer, it appeared that they had not entirely
left the neighbourhood, for instead of one only
being in the neighbourhood of Sussex Square, there
were three of them there.

Morris had ordered the motor to be round that
morning at eleven, and it had been at the door
some few minutes before he appeared. Martin had
driven it round from the stables, but he was in a suit
of tweed; it seemed that he was not going with it.
Then the front door opened, and Morris appeared
as usual in a violent hurry. One of the strangers
was on the pavement close to the house-door,
looking with interest at the car. But his interest in

the car ceased when the boy appeared. And from the railings of the square garden opposite another stranger crossed the road, and from the left behind the car came a third.

'Mr Morris Assheton?' said the first.

'Well, what then?' asked Morris.

The two others moved a little nearer.

'I arrest you in the King's name,' said the first.

Morris was putting on a light coat as he came across the pavement. One arm was in, the other out. He stopped dead; and the bright colour of his face slowly faded, leaving a sort of ashen grey behind. His mouth suddenly went dry, and it was only at the third attempt to speak that words came.

'What for?' he said.

'For the murder of Godfrey Mills,' said the man. 'Here is the warrant. I warn you that all you say——'

Morris, whose lithe athletic frame had gone slack for the moment, stiffened himself up again.

'I am not going to say anything,' he said. 'Martin, drive to Mr Taynton's at once, and tell him that I am arrested.'

The other two now had closed round him.

'Oh, I'm not going to bolt,' he said. 'Please tell me where you are going to take me.'

'Police Court in Branksome Street,' said the first.

'Tell Mr Taynton I am there,' said Morris to his man.

There was a cab at the corner of the square, and in answer to an almost imperceptible nod from one of the men, it moved up to the house. The square was otherwise nearly empty, and Morris looked round as the cab drew nearer. Upstairs in the house he had just left, was his mother who was coming out to Falmer this evening to dine; above illimitable blue stretched from horizon to horizon, behind was the free fresh sea. Birds chirped in the bushes and lilac was in flower. Everything had its liberty.

Then a new instinct seized him, and though a moment before he had given his word that he was not meditating escape, liberty called to him. Everything else was free. He rushed forward, striking right and left with his arms, then tripped on the edge of the paving stones and fell. He was instantly seized, and next moment was in the cab, and fetters of steel, though he could not remember their having been placed there, were on his wrists.

Chapter X

IT WAS a fortnight later, a hot July morning, and an unusual animation reigned in the staid and leisurely streets of Lewes. For the Assizes opened that day, and it was known that the first case to be tried was the murder of which all Brighton and a large part of England had been talking so much since Morris Assheton had been committed for trial. At the hearing in the police-court there was not very much evidence brought forward, but there had been sufficient to make it necessary that he should stand his trial. It was known, for instance, that he had some very serious reason for anger and resentment against his victim; those who had seen him that day remembered him as being utterly unlike himself; he was known to have been at Falmer Park that afternoon about six, and to have driven home along the Falmer Road in his car an hour or so later. And in a copse close by to where the body of the murdered man was found had been discovered a thick bludgeon of a stick, broken it would seem by some violent act, into two halves.

On the top half was rudely cut with a pen-knife M. ASSHE . . . What was puzzling, however, was the apparent motive of robbery about the crime; it will be remembered that the victim's watch was missing, and that no money was found on him.

But since Morris had been brought up for committal at the police-court it was believed that a quantity more evidence of a peculiarly incriminating kind had turned up. Yet in spite of this, so it was rumoured, the prisoner apparently did more than bear up; it was said that he was quite cheerful, quite confident that his innocence would be established. Others said that he was merely callous and utterly without any moral sense. Much sympathy of course was felt for his mother, and even more for the family of the Templetons and the daughter to whom it was said that Morris was actually engaged. And, as much as anyone it was Mr Taynton who was the recipient of the respectful pity of the British public. Though no relation he had all his life been a father to Morris, and while Miss Madge Templeton was young and had the spring and elasticity of youth, so that, though all this was indeed terrible enough, she might be expected to get over it, Mr Taynton was advanced in years and it seemed that he was utterly broken by the shock. He had not been in Brighton on the day on which Morris was brought before the police-court magistrates, and the news had reached him in London after his young friend had been committed. It was said he had fainted straight off, and there had been much difficulty in bringing him round. But since then he had worked day and night on behalf of the accused. But certain fresh evidence which had turned up a day or two before the Assizes seemed to have taken the heart out of him. He had felt confident that the watch would have been found, and the thief traced. But something new that had turned up had utterly staggered him. He could only cling to one hope, and that was that he knew the evidence about the stick must break down, for it was he who had thrown the fragments into the bushes, a fact which would come to light in his own evidence. But at the most, all he could hope for was, that though it seemed as if the poor lad must be condemned, the jury, on account of his youth, and the provocation he had received, of which Mr Taynton would certainly make the most when called upon to bear witness on this point, or owing to some weakness in the terrible chain of evidence that had been woven, would recommend him to mercy.

The awful formalities at the opening of the case were gone through. The judge took his seat, and laid on the bench in front of him a small parcel wrapped up in tissue paper; the jury was sworn in, and the prisoner asked if he objected to the inclusion of any of those among the men who were going to decide whether he was worthy of life or guilty of death, and the packed court, composed about equally of men and women, most of whom would have shuddered to see a dog beaten, or a tired hare made to go an extra mile, settled themselves in their places with a rustle of satisfaction at the thought of seeing a man brought before them in the shame of suspected murder, and promised themselves an interesting and thrilling couple of days in observing the gallows march nearer him, and in watching his mental agony. They who would, and perhaps did, subscribe to benevolent institutions for the relief of suffering among the lower animals, would willingly have paid a far higher rate to observe the suffering of a man. He was so interesting; he was so young and good-looking; what a depraved monster he must be. And that little package in tissue paper which the judge brought in and laid on the bench! The black cap, was it not? That showed what the judge thought about it all. How thrilling!

Counsel for the Crown opened the case, and in a speech grimly devoid of all emotional appeal, laid before the court the facts he was prepared to prove, on which they would base their verdict.

The prisoner, a young man of birth and breeding, had strong grounds for revenge on the murdered man. The prosecution, however, was not concerned in defending what the murdered man had done, but in establishing the guilt of the man who had murdered him. Godfrey Mills had, as could be proved by witnesses, slandered the prisoner in an abominable manner, and the prosecution were not intending for a moment to attempt to establish the truth of his slander. But this slander they put forward as a motive that gave rise to a murderous impulse on the part of the prisoner. The jury would hear from one of the witnesses, an old friend of the prisoner's, and a man who had been a sort of father to him, that a few hours only before the murder was committed the prisoner had uttered certain words which admitted only of one interpretation, namely that murder was in his mind. That the provocation was great was not denied; it was certain, however, that the provocation was sufficient.

Counsel then sketched the actual circumstances of the crime, as far as they could be constructed from what evidence there was. This evidence was purely circumstantial, but of a sort which left no reasonable doubt that the murder had been committed by the prisoner in the manner suggested. Mr Godfrey Mills had gone to London on the Tuesday of the fatal week, intending to return on the Thursday. On the Wednesday the prisoner became cognisant of the fact that Mr Godfrey Mills had — he would not argue over it — wantonly slandered him to Sir Richard Templeton, a marriage with the daughter of whom was projected in the prisoner's mind, which there was reason to suppose might have taken place. Should the jury not be satisfied on that point, witnesses would be called, including the young lady herself, but unless the counsel for the defence challenged their statement, namely that this slander had been spoken which contributed, so it was argued, a motive for the crime, it would be unnecessary to intrude on the poignant and private grief of persons so situated, and to insist on a scene which must prove to be so heart-rendingly painful.

(There was a slight movement of demur in the humane and crowded court at this; it was just

these heart-rendingly painful things which were
so thrilling.)

It was most important, continued counsel for the
prosecution, that the jury should fix these dates
accurately in their minds. Tuesday was June 21st;
it was on that day the murdered man had gone to
London, designing to return on June 23d, Thursday.
The prisoner had learned on Wednesday (June 22d)
that aspersions had been made, false aspersions,
on his character, and it was on Thursday that he
learned for certain from the lips of the man to
whom they had been made, who was the author
of them. The author was Mr Godfrey Mills. He had
thereupon motored back from Falmer Park, and
informed Mr Taynton of this, and had left again for
Falmer an hour later to make an appointment for
Mr Taynton to see Sir Richard. He knew, too, this
would be proved, that Mr Godfrey Mills proposed
to return from London that afternoon, to get out
at Falmer station and walk back to Brighton. It was
certain from the finding of the body that Mr Mills
had travelled from London, as he intended, and
that he had got out at this station. It was certain
also that at that hour the prisoner, burning for
vengeance, and knowing the movements of Mr
Mills, was in the vicinity of Falmer.

To proceed, it was certain also that the prisoner in
a very strange wild state had arrived at Mr Taynton's
house about nine that evening, knowing that Mr
Mills was expected there at about 9.30. Granted
that he had committed the murder, this proceeding
was dictated by the most elementary instinct of self-

preservation. It was also in accordance with that that he had gone round in the pelting rain late that night to see if the missing man had returned to his flat, and that he had gone to London next morning to seek him there. He had not, of course, found him, and he returned to Brighton that afternoon. In connection with this return, another painful passage lay before them, for it would be shown by one of the witnesses that again on the Friday afternoon the prisoner had visited the scene of the crime. Mr Taynton, in fact, still unsuspicious of anything being wrong had walked over the downs that afternoon from Brighton to Falmer, and had sat down in view of the station where he proposed to catch a train back to Brighton, and had seen the prisoner stop his motor-car close to the corner where the body had been found, and behave in a manner inexplicable except on the theory that he knew where the body lay. Subsequently to the finding of the body, which had occurred on Saturday evening, there had been discovered in a coppice adjoining a heavy bludgeon-like stick broken in two. The top of it, which would be produced, bore the inscription M. ASSHE . . .

Mr Taynton was present in court, and was sitting on the bench to the right of the judge who had long been a personal friend of his. Hitherto his face had been hidden in his hands, as this terribly logical tale went on. But here he raised it, and smiled, a wan smile enough, at Morris. The latter did not seem to notice the action. Counsel for the prosecution continued.

All this, he said, had been brought forward at the trial before the police-court magistrates, and he thought the jury would agree that it was more than sufficient to commit the prisoner to trial. At that trial, too, they had heard, the whole world had heard, of the mystery of the missing watch, and the missing money. No money, at least, had been found on the body; it was reasonable to refer to it as 'missing'. But here again, the motive of self-preservation came in; the whole thing had been carefully planned; the prisoner, counsel suggested, had, just as he had gone up to town to find Mr Mills the day after the murder was committed, striven to put justice off the scent in making it appear that the motive for the crime had been robbery. With well-calculated cunning he had taken the watch, and what coins there were, from the pockets of his victim. That at any rate was the theory suggested by the prosecution.

The speech was admirably delivered, and its virtue was its extreme impassiveness; it seemed quite impersonal, the mere automatic action of justice, not revengeful, not seeking for death, but merely tating the case as it might be stated by some planet or remote fixed star. Then there was a short pause, while the prosecutor for the Crown laid down his notes. And the same slow, clear, impassive voice went on.

'But since the committal of the prisoner to stand his trial at these assizes,' he said, 'more evidence of an utterly unexpected, but to us convincing kind has been discovered. Here it is.' And he held up a sheet of blotting paper, and a crumpled envelope.

'A letter has been blotted on this sheet,' he said, 'and by holding it up to the light and looking through it, one can of course, read what was written. But before I read it, I will tell you from where this sheet was taken. It was taken from a blotting book in the drawing-room of Mrs Assheton's house in Sussex Square. An expert in handwriting will soon tell the gentlemen of the jury in whose hand he without doubt considers it to be written. After the committal of the prisoner to trial, search was of course made in this house, for further evidence. This evidence was almost immediately discovered. After that no further search was made.'

The judge looked up from his notes.

'By whom was this discovery made?' he asked.

'By Superintendent Figgis and Sergeant Wilkinson, my lord. They will give their evidence.'

He waited till the judge had entered this.

'I will read the letter,' he said, 'from the negative, so to speak, of the blotting paper.'

June 21st.

To GODFREY MILLS, ESQ.

You damned brute, I will settle you. I hear you are coming back to Brighton tomorrow, and are getting out at Falmer. All right; I shall be there, and we shall have a talk.

MORRIS ASSHETON.

A sort of purr went round the court; the kind humane ladies and gentlemen who had fought for seats found this to their taste. The noose tightened.

'I have here also an envelope,' said the prosecutor, 'which was found by Mr Figgis and Mr Wilkinson in the waste-paper basket in the sitting-room of the deceased. According to the expert in handwriting, whose evidence you will hear, it is undoubtedly addressed by the same hand that wrote the letter I have just read you. And, in his opinion, the handwriting is that of the prisoner. No letter was found in the deceased man's room corresponding to this envelope, but the jury will observe that what I have called the negative of the letter on the blotting paper was dated June 21st, the day that the prisoner suspected the slander that had been levelled at him. The suggestion is that the deceased opened this before leaving for London, and took the letter with him. And the hand, that for the purposes of misleading justice, robbed him of his watch and his money, also destroyed the letter which was then on his person, and which was an incriminating document. But this sheet of blotting paper is as valuable as the letter itself. It proves the letter to have been written.'

Morris had been given a seat in the dock, and on each side of him there stood a prison-warder. But in the awed hush that followed, for the vultures and carrion crows who crowded the court were finding themselves quite beautifully thrilled, he wrote a few words on a slip of paper and handed it to a warder to give to his counsel. And his counsel nodded to him.

The opening speech for the Crown had lasted something over two hours, and a couple of witnesses only were called before the interval for lunch. But most of the human ghouls had brought sandwiches with them, and the court was packed with the same people when Morris was brought up again after the interval, and the judge, breathing sherry, took his seat. The court had become terribly hot, but the public were too humane to mind that. A criminal was being chased toward the gallows, and they followed his progress there with breathless interest. Step by step all that was laid down in the opening speech for the prosecution was inexorably proved, all, that is to say, except the affair of the stick. But from what a certain witness (Mr Taynton) swore to, it was clear that this piece of circumstantial evidence, which indeed was of the greatest importance since the Crown's case was that the murder had been committed with that bludgeon of a stick, completely broke down. Whoever had done the murder, he had not done it with that stick, since Mr Taynton deposed to having been at Mrs Assheton's house on the Friday, the day after the murder had been committed, and to having taken the stick away by mistake, believing it to be his. And the counsel for the defence only asked one question on this point, which question closed the proceedings for the day. It was:

'You have a similar stick then?'

And Mr Taynton replied in the affirmative.
The court then rose.

On the whole the day had been most satisfactory
to the ghouls and vultures and it seemed probable
that they would have equally exciting and plentiful
fare next day. But in the opinion of many Morris's
counsel was disappointing. He did not cross-
examine witnesses at all sensationally, and drag
out dreadful secrets (which had nothing to do with
the case) about their private lives, in order to show
that they seldom if ever spoke the truth. Indeed,
witness after witness was allowed to escape without
any cross-examination at all; there was no attempt
made to prove that the carpenter who had found
the body had been himself tried for murder, or that
his children were illegitimate. Yet gradually, as the
afternoon went on, a sort of impression began to
make its way, that there was something coming
which no one suspected.

The next morning those impressions were
realised when the adjourned cross-examination
of Mr Taynton was resumed. The counsel for the
defence made an immediate attack on the theories
of the prosecution, and it told. For the prosecution
had suggested that Morris's presence at the scene
of the murder the day after was suspicious, as if
he had come back uneasily and of an unquiet
conscience. If that was so, Mr Taynton's presence
there, who had been the witness who proved the
presence of the other, was suspicious also. What
had he come there for? In order to throw the

broken pieces of Morris's stick into the bushes? These inferences were of course but suggested in the questions counsel asked Mr Taynton in the further cross-examination of this morning, and perhaps no one in court saw what the suggestion was for a moment or two, so subtly and covertly was it conveyed. Then it appeared to strike all minds together, and a subdued rustle went round the court, followed the moment after by an even intenser silence.

Then followed a series of interrogations, which at first seemed wholly irrelevant, for they appeared to bear only on the business relations between the prisoner and the witness. Then suddenly like the dim light at the end of a tunnel, where shines the pervading illuminating sunlight, a little ray dawned.

'You have had control of the prisoner's private fortune since 1886?'

'Yes.'

'In the year 1896 he had £8,000 or thereabouts in London and North-Western Debentures, £6,000 in Consols, £7,000 in Government bonds of South Australia?'

'I have no doubt those figures are correct.'

'A fortnight ago you bought £8,000 of London and North-Western Debentures, £6,000 in Consols, £7,000 in Government bonds of South Australia?'

Mr Taynton opened his lips to speak, but no sound came from them.

'Please answer the question.'

If there had been a dead hush before, succeeding the rustle that had followed the suggestions about the stick, a silence far more palpable now descended. There was no doubt as to what the suggestion was now.

The counsel for the prosecution broke in.

'I submit that these questions are irrelevant, my lord,' he said.

'I shall subsequently show, my lord, that they are not.'

'The witness must answer the question,' said the judge. 'I see that there is a possible relevancy.'

The question was answered.

'Thank you, that is all,' said the counsel for the defence, and Mr Taynton left the witness box.

It was then, for the first time since the trial began, that Morris looked at this witness. All through he had been perfectly calm and collected, a circumstance which the spectators put down to the callousness with which they kindly credited him, and now for the first time, as Mr Taynton's eyes and his met, an emotion crossed the prisoner's face. He looked sorry.

Chapter XI

FOR the rest of the morning the examination of witnesses for the prosecution went on, for there were a very large number of them, but when the court rose for lunch, the counsel for the prosecution intimated that this was his last. But again, hardly any but those engaged officially, the judge, the counsel, the prisoner, the warder, left the court. Mr Taynton, however, went home, for he had his seat on the bench, and he could escape for an hour from this very hot and oppressive atmosphere. But he did not go to his Lewes office, or to any hotel to get his lunch. He went to the station, where after waiting some quarter of an hour, he took the train to Brighton. The train ran through Falmer and from his window he could see where the park palings made an angle close to the road; it was from there that the path over the downs, where he had so often walked, passed to Brighton.

Again the judge took his seat, still carrying the little parcel wrapped up in tissue paper.

There was no need for the usher to call silence,

for the silence was granted without being asked
for.

The counsel for the defence called the first
witness; he also unwrapped a flat parcel which
he had brought into court with him, and handed
it to the witness.

'That was supplied by your firm?'

'Yes, sir.'

'Who ordered it?'

'Mr Assheton.'

'Mr Morris Assheton, that is. Did he order it
from you, you yourself?'

'Yes, sir.'

'Did he give any specific instructions about it?'

'Yes, sir.'

'What were they?'

'That the blotting book which Mrs Assheton
had already ordered was to be countermanded,
and that this was to be sent in its stead on June
24th.'

'You mean not after June 24th?'

'No, sir; the instructions were that it was not to
be sent before June 24th.'

'Why was that?'

'I could not say, sir. Those were the
instructions.'

'And it was sent on June 24th.'

'Yes, sir. It was entered in our book.'

The book in question was produced and handed
to the jury and the judge.

'That is all. Mrs Assheton.'

She stepped into the box, and smiled at Morris.

There was no murmur of sympathy, no rustling; the whole thing was too tense.

'You returned home on June 24th last, from a visit to town?'

'Yes.'

'At what time?'

'I could not say to the minute. But about eleven in the morning.'

'You found letters waiting for you?'

'Yes.'

'Anything else?'

'A parcel.'

'What did it contain?'

'A blotting book. It was a present from my son on my birthday.'

'Is this the blotting book?'

'Yes.'

'What did you do with it?'

'I opened it and placed it on my writing-table in the drawing-room.'

'Thank you; that is all.'

There was no cross-examination of this witness, and after the pause, the counsel for the defence spoke again.

'Superintendent Figgis. You searched the house of Mrs Assheton in Sussex Square?'

'Yes, sir.'

'What did you take from it?'

'A leaf from a blotting book, sir.'

'Was it that leaf which has been already produced in court, bearing the impress of a letter dated June 21st?'

'Yes, sir.'

'Where was the blotting book?'

'On the writing-table in the drawing-room, sir.'

'You did not examine the blotting book in any way?'

'No, sir.'

Counsel opened the book and fitted the torn out leaf into its place.

'We have here the impress of a letter dated June 21st, written in a new blotting book that did not arrive at Mrs Assheton's house from the shop till June 24th. It threatens — threatens a man who was murdered, supposedly by the prisoner, on June 23d. Yet this threatening letter was not written till June 24th, after he had killed him.'

Quiet and unemotional as had been the address for the Crown, these few remarks were even quieter. Then the examination continued.

'You searched also the flat occupied by the deceased, and you found there this envelope, supposedly in the handwriting of the prisoner, which has been produced by the prosecution?'

'Yes, sir.'

'This is it?'

'Yes, sir.'

'Thank you. That is all.'

Again there was no cross-examination, and the superintendent left the witness box.

Then the counsel for the defence took up two blank envelopes in addition to the one already produced and supposedly addressed in the handwriting of the prisoner.

'This blue envelope,' he said, 'is from the stationery in Mrs Assheton's house. This other envelope, white, is from the flat of the deceased. It corresponds in every way with the envelope which was supposed to be addressed in the prisoner's hand, found at the flat in question. The inference is that the prisoner blotted the letter dated June 21st on a blotting pad which did not arrive in Mrs Assheton's house till June 24th, went to the deceased's flat and put it in an envelope there.

These were handed to the jury for examination.

'Ernest Smedley,' said counsel.

Mills's servant stepped into the box, and was sworn.

'Between, let us say June 21st and June 24th, did the prisoner call at Mr Mills's flat?'

'Yes, sir, twice.'

'When?'

'Once on the evening of June 23d, and once very early next morning.'

'Did he go in?'

'Yes, sir, he came in on both occasions.'

'What for?'

'To satisfy himself that Mr Mills had not come back.'

'Did he write anything?'

'No, sir.'

'How do you know that?'

'I went with him from room to room, and should have seen if he had done so.'

'Did anybody else enter the flat during those days?'

'Yes, sir.'

'Who?'

'Mr Taynton.'

The whole court seemed to give a great sigh; then it was quiet again. The judge put down the pen with which he had been taking notes, and like the rest of the persons present he only listened.

'When did Mr Taynton come into the flat?'

'About mid-day or a little later on Friday.'

'June 24th?'

'Yes, sir.'

'Please tell the jury what he did?'

The counsel for the prosecution stood up.

'I object to that question,' he said.

The judge nodded at him; then looked at the witness again. The examination went on.

'You need not answer that question. I put it to save time, merely. Did Mr Taynton go into the deceased's sitting-room?'

'Yes, sir.'

'Did he write anything there?'

'Yes, sir.'

'Was he alone there?'

'Yes, sir.'

'Thank you.'

Again the examining counsel paused, and again no question was asked by the prosecution.

'Charles Martin,' said the counsel for defence.

'You are a servant of the prisoner's?'

'Yes, sir.'

'You were in his service during this week of June, of which Friday was June 24th?'

'Yes, sir.'

'Describe the events— No. Did the prisoner go up to town, or elsewhere on that day, driving his motor-car, but leaving you in Brighton?'

'Yes, sir.'

'Mrs Assheton came back that morning?'

'Yes, sir.'

'Did anyone call that morning? If so, who.'

'Mr Taynton called.'

'Did he go to the drawing-room?'

'Yes, sir.'

'Did he write anything there?'

'Yes, sir; he wrote a note to Mrs Assheton, which he gave me when he went out.'

'You were not in the drawing-room, when he wrote it?'

'No, sir.'

'Did he say anything to you when he left the house?'

'Yes, sir.'

'What did he say?'

The question was not challenged now.

'He told me to say that he had left the note at the door.'

'But he had not done so?'

'No, sir; he wrote it in the drawing-room.

'Thank you. That is all.'

But this witness was not allowed to pass as the others had done. The counsel for the prosecution got up.

'You told Mrs Assheton that it had been left at the door?'

'Yes, sir.'

'You knew that was untrue?'

'Yes, sir.'

'For what reason did you say it, then?'

Martin hesitated; he looked down, then he looked up again, and was still silent.

'Answer the question.'

His eyes met those of the prisoner. Morris smiled at him, and nodded.

'Mr Taynton told me to say that,' he said, 'I had once been in Mr Taynton's service. He dismissed me. I——'

The judge interposed looking at the cross-examining counsel.

'Do you press your question?' he asked. 'I do not forbid you to ask it, but I ask you whether the case for the prosecution of the — the prisoner is furthered by your insisting on this question. We have all heard, the jury and I alike, what the last three or four witnesses have said, and you have allowed that — quite properly, in my opinion — to go unchallenged. I do not myself see that there is anything to be gained by the prosecution by pressing the question. I ask you to consider this point. If you think conscientiously, that the evidence, the trend of which we all know now, is to be shaken, you are right to do your best to try to shake it. If not, I wish you to consider whether you should press the question. What the result of your pressing it will be, I have no idea, but it is certainly clear to us all now, that there was a threat implied in Mr Taynton's words. Personally I do not wish to know what that threat was, nor do I see how the knowledge of it would affect your case in my eyes, or in the eyes of the jury.'

There was a moment's pause.

'No, my lord, I do not press it.'

Then a clear young voice broke the silence.

'Thanks, Martin,' it said.

It came from the dock.

The judge looked across to the dock for a moment, with a sudden irresistible impulse of kindliness for the prisoner whom he was judging.

'Charles Martin,' he said, 'you have given your evidence, and speaking for myself, I believe it to be entirely trustworthy. I wish to say that your character is perfectly clear. No aspersion whatever has been made on it, except that you said a note had been delivered at the door, though you knew it to have been not so delivered. You made that statement through fear of a certain individual; you were frightened into telling a lie. No one inquires into the sources of your fear.'

But in the general stillness, there was one part of the court that was not still, but the judge made no command of silence there, for in the jury-box there was whispering and consultation. It went on for some three minutes. Then the foreman of the jury stood up.

'The jury have heard sufficient of this case, my lord,' he said, 'and they are agreed on their verdict.'

For a moment the buzzing whispers went about the court again, shrilling high, but instantaneously they died down, and the same tense silence prevailed. But from the back of the court there was a stir, and the judge seeing what it was that caused it waited, while Mrs Assheton moved from her place, and made her way to the front of the dock in which Morris sat. She had been in the witness-box that day, and everyone knew her, and all made way for her, moving as the blades of corn move when the wind stirs them, for her right was recognised and unquestioned. But the dock was high above her, and a barrister who sat below instantly vacated his seat, she got up and stood on it. All eyes were fixed on her, and none saw that at this moment a telegram was handed to the judge which he opened and read.

Then he turned to the foreman of the jury.

'What verdict do you find?' he asked.

'Not guilty.'

Mrs Assheton had already grasped Morris's hands in hers, and just as the words were spoken she kissed him.

Then a shout arose which bade fair to lift the roof off, and neither judge nor ushers of the court made any attempt to quiet it, and if it was only for the sensation of seeing the gallows march nearer the prisoner that these folk had come together, yet there was no mistaking the genuineness of their congratulations now. Morris's whole behaviour, too, had been so gallant and brave; innocent though he knew himself to be, yet it required a very high courage to listen to the damning accumulation of evidence against him and if there is one thing that the ordinary man appreciates more than sensation, it is pluck. Then, but not for a long time, the uproar subsided, and the silence descended again. Then the judge spoke.

'Mr Assheton,' he said, 'for I no longer can call you prisoner, the jury have of course found you not guilty of the terrible crime of which you were accused, and I need not say that I entirely agree with their verdict. Throughout the trial you have had my sympathy and my admiration for your gallant bearing.' Then at a sign from the judge his mother and he were let out by the private door below the bench.

After they had gone silence was restored. Everyone knew that there must be more to come. The prisoner was found not guilty; the murder was still unavenged.

Then once more the judge spoke.

'I wish to make public recognition,' he said, 'of the fairness and ability with which the case was conducted on both sides. The prosecution, as it was their duty to do, forged the chain of evidence against Mr Assheton as strongly as they were able, and pieced together incriminating circumstances against him with a skill that at first seemed conclusive of his guilt. The first thing that occurred to make a weak link in their chain was the acknowledgement of a certain witness that the stick with which the murder was supposed to have been committed was not left on the spot by the accused, but by himself. Why he admitted that we can only conjecture, but my conjecture is that it was an act of repentance and contrition on his part. When it came to that point he could not let the evidence which he had himself supplied tell against him on whom it was clearly his object to father the crime. You will remember also that certain circumstances pointed to robbery being the motive of the crime. That I think was the first idea, so to speak, of the real criminal. Then, we must suppose, he saw himself safer, if he forged against another certain evidence which we have heard.'

The judge paused for a moment, and then went on with evident emotion.

'This case will never be reopened again,' he said, 'for a reason that I will subsequently tell the court; we have seen the last of this tragedy, and retribution and punishment are in the hands of a higher and supreme tribunal. This witness, Mr Edward Taynton — has been for years a friend of mine, and the sympathy which I felt for him at the opening of the case, when a young man, to whom I still believe him to have been attached, was on his trial, is changed to a deeper pity. During the afternoon you have heard certain evidence, from which you no doubt as well as I infer that the fact of this murder having been committed was known to the man who wrote a letter and blotted it on the sheet which has been before the court. That man also, as it was clear to us an hour ago, directed a certain envelope which you have also seen. I may add that Mr Taynton had, as I knew, an extraordinary knack of imitating handwritings; I have seen him write a signature that I could have sworn was mine. But he has used that gift for tragic purposes.

I have just received a telegram. He left this court before the luncheon interval, and went to his house in Brighton. Arrived there, as I have just learned, he poisoned himself. And may God have mercy on his soul.'

Again he paused.

'The case therefore is closed,' he said, 'and the court will rise for the day. You will please go out in silence.'

MORE VINTAGE MURDER MYSTERIES

MARGERY ALLINGHAM
Mystery Mile
Police at the Funeral
Sweet Danger
Flowers for the Judge
The Case of the Late Pig
The Fashion in Shrouds
Traitor's Purse
Coroner's Pidgin
More Work for the Undertaker
The Tiger in the Smoke
The Beckoning Lady
Hide My Eyes
The China Governess
The Mind Readers
Cargo of Eagles

E. F. BENSON
The Blotting Book
The Luck of the Vails

NICHOLAS BLAKE
A Question of Proof
Thou Shell of Death
There's Trouble Brewing
The Beast Must Die
The Smiler With the Knife
Malice in Wonderland
The Case of the Abominable Snowman
Minute for Murder
Head of a Traveller
The Dreadful Hollow
The Whisper in the Gloom
End of Chapter
The Widow's Cruise
The Worm of Death
The Sad Variety
The Morning After Death

EDMUND CRISPIN
Buried for Pleasure
The Case of the Gilded Fly
Holy Disorders
Love Lies Bleeding
The Moving Toyshop
Swan Song

A. A. MILNE
The Red House Mystery

GLADYS MITCHELL
Speedy Death
The Mystery of a Butcher's Shop
The Longer Bodies
The Saltmarsh Murders
Death at the Opera
The Devil at Saxon Wall
Dead Men's Morris
Come Away, Death
St Peter's Finger
Brazen Tongue
Hangman's Curfew
When Last I Died
Laurels Are Poison
Here Comes a Chopper
Death and the Maiden
Tom Brown's Body
Groaning Spinney
The Devil's Elbow
The Echoing Strangers
Watson's Choice
The Twenty-Third Man
Spotted Hemlock
My Bones Will Keep
Three Quick and Five Dead
Dance to Your Daddy
A Hearse on May-Day
Late, Late in the Evening
Fault in the Structure
Nest of Vipers